Designed by Brigitte Willgoss
Stories compiled and edited by Debbie Lines

ISBN 0 86112 561 4
© Brimax Books Ltd 1989. All rights reserved.
Published by Brimax Books Ltd, Newmarket, England 1989
Printed in Spain

A Collection of
CLASSIC
FAIRY TALES

Illustrated by Christa Hook
Jonathon Heap

Brimax Books · Newmarket · England

Contents

Cinderella

Once upon a time there lived a rich merchant. He was a widower and he had a beautiful young daughter.

One day he took a new wife. This wife already had two daughters, Drusilla and Esmerelda. Both were ugly and were very jealous of their new step-sister.

Soon after they arrived at the merchant's house, the merchant had to go on a long business trip. While he was away, things changed for his young daughter.

"Does she really have to sit with us in the parlour?" said Drusilla to her mother one day.

"And does she have to eat with us?" added Esmerelda.

Their mother looked at the young girl and said: "If you want to eat bread, then you must earn it. Off to the kitchen with you. You will be the new kitchen maid."

With that the poor girl was taken off to the kitchen where she had to change all her fine clothes for a dress of rags and wooden shoes. From then on, from dawn to dusk, she had to cook, clean, tend the fire, fetch the water and run around after her stepmother and stepsisters. She had to sleep by the fire. Her clothes became so dirty that they decided to call her Cinderella.

But in spite of the ashes and dirt that covered her and her clothes, she was still far prettier than Drusilla and Esmerelda.

One day there was an announcement that the King was going to invite all the young ladies of the kingdom to two balls so that his son could choose a bride.

The invitations arrived at the merchant's house, causing great excitement.

"Of course he'll choose me," said Drusilla as she looked at herself in the mirror.

"He will not!" exclaimed Esmerelda. "I'll be the one he chooses. I'll be his wife and one day I'll be Queen!"

"Mama!" cried Drusilla. "Tell Esmerelda that I'm the oldest and that I shall marry the Prince!"

"Girls, girls," said their mother. "The Prince is sure to choose one of my darling daughters. We'll just let him decide which one and the other one will marry a great Duke or Lord and you'll both be happy."

Then she went to the door. "Cinderella!" she called. When Cinderella arrived, her stepmother said, "My darling daughters have been invited to the King's balls and I'm sure that one will be chosen by the Prince to be his wife. They must be dressed to fit the occasion. I want you to work night and day making new ball gowns for us all."

"Am I invited, too?" asked Cinderella.

"You!" cried her stepmother. "You're nothing but a servant. Why should you be invited? Besides, you have nothing to wear. You would only be an embarrassment to us all!"

From then on Cinderella had to work non-stop on the dresses for her stepmother and stepsisters. Six different ball gowns was quite a task but to try and make her stepsisters look even slightly pretty was nearly impossible.

For two whole days before the first ball, Drusilla and Esmerelda hardly ate because they were so excited and they spent hours in front of their mirrors. They spent even more time trying to tie the laces on their dresses tighter to make their waists smaller. Cinderella was a kind-hearted girl and she tried her hardest to make their frizzy hair stay neat and tidy and to make their faces look pretty. But really it was a hopeless task.

The evening of the ball came and the three ladies were ready at last. Cinderella watched as they left. Only when they were out of sight did she begin to cry.

"Oh, I did so want to go to the ball," she wept.

"And so you shall," said a voice behind her.

Turning round, Cinderella came face to face with a strange lady who had appeared from nowhere. She held a wand. Her dress twinkled and glittered.

"I am your fairy godmother," she said.

"My fairy godmother!" cried Cinderella. "I didn't know I had one!"

"Oh, everyone has one," said the strange lady. "But not many people get to know theirs. Now, be a good girl and fetch me a pumpkin, a white rat, six white mice and two green lizards."

Cinderella went off to the garden and soon came back with what her fairy godmother had asked for.

"Now stand back, and let's see what we can do, shall we," said the fairy godmother.

Cinderella looked on as her fairy godmother tapped the pumpkin with her wand. To her amazement, it grew and grew and twinkled and shone until standing there was a beautiful golden coach.

"Now for the horses," said the fairy godmother and she turned to the six white mice. She tapped them with her wand and in a moment, there before them were six white horses harnessed to the coach.

"You'll need a driver, of course, and footmen," said the fairy godmother. "And that's where these come in." She tapped the rat and the lizards and they were instantly turned into a smiling fat coachman and two footmen, all in green and gold livery.

"There," said the fairy godmother, "you're ready to go now."

"But I've nothing to wear," said Cinderella, sadly.

"Really! Well, what are you wearing now, child?" asked her fairy godmother.

"I can't go in these," said Cinderella. "They're nothing but rags." She looked down at herself and what she saw took her breath away. While she had been watching what her fairy godmother was doing, her rags had been changed into the most beautiful dress of silver material and on her feet were the daintiest pair of silver shoes.

"Now then," said her fairy godmother, smiling. "You must be home by midnight for the magic stops then. Now off you go, and have a lovely time."

"Oh, thank you so much, fairy godmother," said Cinderella. "I promise I'll be home by midnight."

She got into the coach which swept her off to the ball.

When she arrived, silence fell in the hall. No one had ever seen so beautiful a girl, and no one knew who she was. Even her stepmother and stepsisters didn't recognise her. The Prince was enchanted and would let no one else dance with her. He sat by her at the feast and would not let her out of his sight.

Cinderella was enjoying herself so much that she did not notice the time slipping by. Suddenly the clock struck a quarter to midnight.

"I must go," she said to the Prince and before he had a chance to say anything she had run from the room.

The coach took her home and at the stroke of midnight, the magic ended and the coach turned back into a pumpkin and the rat, mice and lizards ran off into the fields.

When her stepmother and stepsisters arrived home a while later,

all they could talk about was the mysterious girl.

"She must have been a princess," said Drusilla.

"She must have been a foreign princess," said Esmerelda. "You should have seen her, Cinderella. She was quite pretty, as Princesses go, but naturally, not as pretty as either of us."

"And her dress," said Drusilla. "It was silver . . ."

"With jewels on it," interrupted Esmerelda.

"I'm surprised that the Prince was allowed to pay so much attention to her, though," said their mother. "Especially when there were two more beautiful girls waiting to talk to him. Cinderella, tomorrow my two darling girls must be absolutely exquisite for the ball."

Cinderella smiled and said: "Of course, Stepmother, I'll do everything I can."

Turning to her daughters again, the stepmother ushered them out of the room. "Now, girls, off to bed with you," she said. "We don't want to lose any beauty sleep, do we?"

The next day, Cinderella worked hard changing things on the gowns to make them even more beautiful. Eventually the time came for the three ladies to leave for the ball.

When they had gone, Cinderella waited for her fairy godmother.

"Well now," said the strange lady as she appeared in front of Cinderella. "Did you enjoy yourself last night? I hope it all went well."

"I had a wonderful time," said Cinderella excitedly. "Thank you so much for letting me go."

"Have you got all the things from yesterday ready?" asked her fairy godmother.

"Yes," said Cinderella. "I collected them while Drusilla and Esmerelda were having their nap."

"Good," said the fairy godmother. "Well, there's not much more to do then."

Again she worked her magic and moments later, the coach and horses were standing before them with the coachman and footmen waiting.

This time Cinderella had a beautiful dress of gold and shoes of sparkling crystal.

"Oh, it's so lovely," cried Cinderella. "Thank you so much!"

"Remember, you must leave before midnight," her fairy godmother reminded her. "Now, enjoy yourself."

The coach took her off to the palace, where she was greeted with great joy by the Prince. He had been waiting for her and for the whole of the evening he danced only with her.

Cinderella was so enjoying herself that the fairy godmother's warning was completely forgotten. Suddenly she heard the first stroke of midnight.

"Is that eleven o'clock?" she asked the Prince while they were dancing.

"No," he said. "That's the first stroke of twelve."

"Twelve!" cried Cinderella. "Oh, no!" And she gave a very quick curtsey and ran from the room. She ran down and down the palace steps hearing the clock strike twelve in the tower. As she ran her clothes began to change and were soon turned back into rags. She dropped one of the crystal slippers in her haste, but could not go back for it.

The Prince tried to follow but he could not catch her. All he found was the glass slipper and this he kept and held on to. At the gates the guards were questioned, but all they had seen was a young kitchen maid, not a Princess in a fine coach.

Cinderella arrived home, completely out of breath. Gone were the coach and the horses and the coachman and footmen. Her dress was again dirty rags and she had wooden shoes on her feet.

Soon after Drusilla, Esmerelda and their mother arrived home.

"Was the mysterious girl there again?" asked Cinderella.

"Yes, she was," said Drusilla. "And her behaviour was very strange."

"At the stroke of midnight, she ran off," added Esmerelda.

"All she left behind was her crystal slipper," said Drusilla.

"And the Prince sat and stared at it for the rest of the evening," said their mother. "He didn't take the slightest notice of either of these two beautiful girls."

"Oh, Mama," said Drusilla. "Anyone could see that he was in love with the owner of the crystal slipper."

And so it was. For the following day there was an announcement that the Prince would marry the girl whose foot fitted the slipper.

First the Prince took it to the princesses in the kingdom. Then he went to the duchesses and then to the ladies of the court. But nobody could put on the crystal slipper.

"I must take it to all the ladies who were invited to the balls," said the Prince.

Eventually, he arrived at the merchant's house.

"Oh, it will fit my foot," said Drusilla. And she heaved and she pulled at the shoe to make her foot go in but all that would fit in was her big toe.

"It doesn't fit, Drusilla," said Esmerelda. "Give the shoe to me. I'll show you." And she heaved and pulled at the shoe to make her foot go in but it was to no avail, her foot was just too big.

"Is there no one else who can try it on?" asked the Prince.

"Well, there's only the kitchen maid, Cinderella," said the stepmother. "But she wasn't even at the balls, so it can't be hers."

Cinderella was called for. "Shall I try it on," she asked smiling as she recognised the slipper.

Drusilla and Esmerelda laughed. "Try it on, but it won't fit you. It's made for a tiny foot."

Their laughter almost turned to tears when they saw Cinderella's foot slip into the shoe. And they nearly howled when they saw her take the other shoe from her pocket and put that one on too.

Cinderella looked up at the Prince, who immediately recognised her as the girl he had danced with and had fallen in love with.

"This is the girl I shall marry," he declared, taking her by the hand.

Cinderella's stepmother and stepsisters were astounded when they realised that Cinderella was the mysterious girl and they begged her forgiveness.

Cinderella immediately forgave them and the Prince took her off to the palace where they were married a few days later, amid great celebration.

The Frog Prince

Long ago, there once lived a King who had three daughters. The youngest daughter was the most beautiful of the three.

Near the King's palace there was a gloomy forest. In the middle of the forest was a pond with a fountain that gurgled merrily. Nearby stood an old spreading lime tree. The youngest Princess used to spend hours sitting by the cool pond in the forest, especially when the weather was hot.

One particular day, she went to the pond and was playing with her golden ball. She was tossing it into the air and catching it, but after one throw she missed it and it rolled along the ground and into the pond. She watched it disappear beneath the surface.

"Oh, no!" she cried. "I'll never get it back now. The water's far too deep to reach the bottom." She began to cry.

"Why do you cry, Princess?" asked a voice close by. The Princess looked up, and much to her surprise, she saw a frog showing its head above the water.

Again it asked, "Why do you cry, Princess? What's wrong?"

"I've lost my golden ball," said the Princess. "It fell into the pond and must be at the bottom, for I cannot see it."

"Don't cry," said the frog. "I'll get it for you. But what will you give me for fetching it?"

"What would you like?" asked the Princess. "My dresses, my jewels or my golden crown?"

"Your jewels and dresses are not for me," said the frog. "But if you will love me, and be my friend, if you will let me sit at your table, let me eat off your plate and let me sleep in your bed, then I shall fetch the ball for you."

The Princess would do anything to get her ball back and so she agreed to what the frog asked.

The frog then dived down out of sight and soon came up with the ball in his mouth. As soon as he tossed the ball to the Princess, she ran off with it without a backward glance. She forgot about the frog completely.

"Wait for me," called the frog. "I cannot keep up with you." He watched as she ran out of the wood then he turned back and returned to the pond.

The next day, the young Princess was dining with her sisters and her father, and she was eating from her golden plate when all at once, outside in the corridor, a curious noise could be heard: splish-splash, splish-splash. It came up the marble stairs and stopped outside the door.

Then a voice called, "Open the door, youngest Princess."

So she got up and went to see who was calling her. She opened the door and there sat the frog. The Princess slammed the door shut and returned to her seat.

"Who was at the door?" asked her father.

"Only a frog," said the Princess quietly.

"What does a frog want with you?" asked the King.

"I was playing by the pond in the wood and my ball fell in the pond," began the Princess. "The frog fetched it for me but not before he made me promise that I should be his friend. I didn't think frogs left water, but he's here now and he wants to come in."

"And you promised," said her father, "to be his friend?"

"Yes, but . . . " began the Princess.

"No buts, my dear," said the King firmly. "A promise made is a promise to be kept. Go and let him in."

The Princess opened the door and then went back to her seat.

"Pick me up, please," said the frog.

The Princess hesitated but a look from her father made her put the frog onto the chair beside her. He then jumped onto the table.

"Now push the plate over here so I may eat," said the frog.

The frog enjoyed his dinner, but the Princess seemed almost to choke on hers.

"That's much better," said the frog. "I feel quite tired now. Will you take me upstairs so that I may sleep in your bed?"

The Princess was horrified. "Father, I can't do that!" she cried, tears beginning to run down her cheeks.

"You can and you must," said the King. "You promised."

The Princess did not like touching the frog so she picked him up with two fingers and went upstairs to her room. She put the frog in a corner and got into her bed.

As she lay there, the frog crawled up to the bed. "I am tired. Please pick me up and put me on the bed or I shall tell your father."

The Princess leant out of bed and picked up the frog.

"I have let you sit on my chair, I have shared my food with you," she cried. "Must I really let you lie on my bed?" Then she tossed the frog to the end of the bed and buried her face in her hands, so she did not see the magic happen. The frog lay at the end of the bed for a moment and then magically changed to a handsome young man.

"Please don't cry," said the young man.

The Princess looked up in surprise to see the young man on her bed. She looked around the bed and on the floor.

"Where's the frog?" she asked.

"You have broken the spell," said the young man as she looked. "I am a Prince and was enchanted by an evil witch. Only you could break the spell by letting me eat with you and letting me lie on your bed."

The Princess was delighted and soon after she and the Prince were married and returned to his kingdom to live happily for the rest of their lives.

24

The Stolen Turnips

There was once an old man and an old woman who lived in a cottage in a forest. The cottage was a curious building because it had a tower on one corner that could only be reached by a steep narrow staircase and it had a little flat roof. The garden surrounding the cottage was full to the brim with growing fruit and vegetables. Not a pea more could be grown.

Now the old woman was very hard on the old man, insisting that whatever went wrong was his fault. If it rained too much, it was his fault. If the weather was too dry, it was his fault.

One day the old woman took it into her head that she wanted turnips in the garden.

"But there's no room for turnips," said the old man.

"Then sow them on top of the tower," said the old woman. "It has a flat roof."

"But there's no earth up there."

"Then take some up," she cried. "But grow me some turnips!"

So the old man climbed up and down the rickety staircase carrying sacks of earth to spread onto the flat roof. He had to hold the sack in his teeth to carry it, because he needed both hands to help him on the staircase. By evening the earth had been laid and the seeds had been sown.

From then on the old woman made him climb the staircase every day to check on the plants. Eventually the day came when he could say that the turnips were growing and would soon be ready to eat.

One day he climbed back down and his wife was waiting.

"How are they getting on?" she asked.

"Most of them are nearly big enough to eat," he replied. "But I'm afraid that the best ones have been stolen."

"Stolen!" she cried. "What do you mean, stolen? Find out who's done this!"

The old man hurried away. He wandered into the wood, thinking about the thieves. 'They could be birds or squirrels. How could I possibly catch them? Grow wings?'

After he had wandered for some time, he came to a clearing. Near the trees on the far side was a hut. There was such noise coming from it, such chattering and laughing that as he got closer, he had to put his hands over his ears. He thought he saw little faces looking at him through the windows, and peeping round the door. But when he put his foot on the step the noise stopped. He walked into the hut and there was no sign of anyone.

In the corner there was a heap of rags and blankets. But in the middle of the floor was part of a leaf, a turnip leaf. As the old man looked at it, the heap of blankets began to fidget and move. Little giggles came from the pile, then suddenly the blankets were thrown back as dozens of little children leapt up and danced round the old man. Each child had a turnip and showed it to him.

"So it was you," said the old man. "You took the turnips from the top of the tower."

"Yes," they laughed. "We stole the turnips!"

"How did you get up there?" he asked.

They would not tell. They just burst out laughing.

"You may laugh," said the old man. "But I'm the one who is told off."

"Never mind," they chattered. "We'll pay for them."

"But how?"

They chattered and laughed and looked at the old man, then one of them said, "Are you hungry, grandfather?"

"Yes, I am," said the old man. "I've been looking for you all day. And I had to leave without breakfast."

"If you're hungry, open that cupboard." The old man opened the cupboard.

"Take out the tablecloth, and spread it on the table." The old man did so.

"Now we'll sit and eat." And they all sat at the table.

"But there's nothing to eat," said the old man.

The children laughed and said, "Just tell the cloth to turn inside out."

"How?"

"Just say to it, 'tablecloth, turn inside out'," they laughed.

So the old man said in a firm voice, "Tablecloth, turn inside out." And the tablecloth lifted itself, rolled and laid itself flat again, revealing all sorts of food – soups and salads, meat and fish, puddings and cakes.

The children and the old man ate until they had cleared the table.

"Who washes up?" asked the old man.

"No one," they laughed. "Just say tablecloth, turn outside in."

When the old man told the tablecloth to do this, it flipped up, rolled again and then laid itself out flat with not a thing on it.

"Take the tablecloth as payment for the turnips," said the children.

"Thank you, I will," said the old man. He folded the cloth and tucked it carefully away in his pocket. "Goodbye and thank you for the tablecloth."

"Goodbye," chattered the children, "and thank you for the turnips."

The old man wandered home.

"Did you find the thieves?" asked his wife as soon as he appeared.

"Yes, it was a crowd of very strange little children."

"Did you beat them?"

"No," said the old man. "I had dinner with them."

At that the old woman flew into a terrible rage. As she ranted and raved, the old man thought of other quieter things, ignoring his wife's anger. Then he said, "But they paid for the turnips."

"How," she cried. "What do children have?"

"They gave me a tablecloth," he said and he quickly pulled it out and told it to turn inside out. Again, the tablecloth produced a marvellous feast. The old woman stopped short. She smelt the meat, tasted the soups and then settled down to eat. So did the old man.

As soon as she had finished, the old woman said, "But look at all the washing up that leaves me."

"Ah, no," said the old man. "Look," and he told the cloth to turn outside in so that all the dishes and plates disappeared.

"It's not bad," said the old woman. "After all, they did owe me something for those turnips."

That night, while the old man was asleep, the old woman took the tablecloth and hid it and put one of her own in its place.

The next morning the old woman told the old man to go and check the turnips. But he saw the tablecloth on the table and decided to stop for breakfast first.

He said, "Tablecloth, turn inside out." but the tablecloth did not move.

"Ah well," he said and went outside. He told his wife what had happened, that the tablecloth didn't work anymore.

"Well, a tablecloth is a tablecloth, so what did you expect? Now get up the stairs and check my turnips!" ordered the old woman.

When the old man reached the roof, he wondered how he would tell his wife the news. He went slowly back down the stairs.

"Well," she said sharply. "Are they all right?"

"They're doing very well, but there are more missing."

"More stolen! Go and find those children and give them a sound beating."

"Let me have a bite to eat first," said the old man. "It's a long way to go and I've not eaten yet."

"And you'll not eat until I know that no more of my turnips will be stolen. Now be off!" yelled the old woman.

So the old man went off into the forest. As soon as he was out of sight, the old woman got out the real tablecloth and had a fine breakfast.

The old man reached the hut and found the children, each holding a turnip. They laughed when they saw the old man.

"So it was you," he said.

"We stole the turnips," sang the children.

"And I'm the one who is told off," replied the old man.

"Never mind, we'll pay for the turnips."

"That's all very well, but the tablecloth you gave me yesterday does not work today."

At that the children went quiet. Then they chattered quietly.

"We'll give you something better today," one of them said. "We'll give you a goat."

"A goat!"

"Oh, it's special," said the children. "It has a cold." They took him behind the hut where there stood a goat.

"Tell it to sneeze," said one child.

Remembering the tablecloth, the old man bowed to the goat and then said, "Sneeze, goat."

The goat started to sneeze and sneeze and as it sneezed gold pieces flew in all directions.

"Tell it to stop," said the children. "We have no use for all that gold."

"Stop sneezing, goat," said the old man, and the goat stopped. It was surrounded by gold coins which the children were playing with, kicking them into the bushes and grass.

Then the children fed the old man and toward evening he left, leading the goat on a rope. As he went, the children were singing, "Who stole the turnips? We stole the turnips. Who paid for the turnips? We paid for the turnips. Who stole the tablecloth? Who will pay for the tablecloth? Who will steal turnips again? We will steal turnips again!"

But the old man was too pleased with the goat to listen to what the children were saying.

The old woman was waiting at the door for him.

"Have you beaten those children?" she screamed.

"No," said the old man and he quickly added, "but they paid for the turnips."

"With what? What did they give you? Was it with that goat? I have three already, all better than that one!"

"Sneeze, goat," said the old man quickly.

And the goat sneezed and the gold fell in all directions. The old woman scurried around trying to pick it all up. When the goat stopped, the old woman looked up.

"You're too late for supper. I've had mine." She went inside with her little hoard of gold.

The old man tied up the goat so that it could eat good green grass.

That night, as he slept, the old woman exchanged the goat that sneezed gold for one of her ordinary goats. "They were my turnips," she muttered to herself.

The next morning she told the old man to go and check the turnips. He climbed the creaky old stairs and when he reached the top, he was almost afraid to come down again. There were hardly any turnips left.

The scolding the old woman gave him when he reached the ground this time made him scurry away to the woods with his hands over his ears.

This time he reached the woods and found the children playing in the clearing. Each was holding a turnip. They came running up to the old man. "We stole the turnips!" they shouted.

"I know, I know," said the old man. "And it's me who's told off for it."

"Never again," they cried.

"Good, I'm glad to hear it," said the old man.

"And we'll pay for the turnips!"

"Thank you," said the old man. He found he could not scold the children. This time they gave him a whistle.

"I can t play this; my fingers are too old and stiff," said the old man.

"Blow, blow," cried the children, laughing and giggling.

The old man blew, and out of the pipe flew three whips which started to beat him across the head and shoulders.

"Blow again!" shouted the children. "Tell the whips to get into the whistle! Quick!"

34

The old man blew and the whips stopped. "Into the whistle," he said, and the whips disappeared into the whistle.

"Take it home," laughed the children. "That should pay for everything."

"I think you may be right," answered the old man. "Goodbye children."

When he got home, the old woman was counting her gold pieces. She leapt up when she saw him.

"What have those children tricked you with this time?" she screamed.

"A whistle," he replied. "And they're not going to take any more turnips."

"A whistle!" screamed the old woman. "What's the good of that? Give it to me. They were my turnips."

"Whatever you do, don't blow it," warned the old man.

"What, not blow my own whistle." And the old woman took the whistle and blew.

Out flew the three whips and they started to beat her.

"Stop them! Stop them!" she cried. "I'm sorry I scold so much! I stole the tablecloth – it's in the chest. The goat is behind the shed. Please stop them!" The old man tried to grab the whistle, but the old woman was running around so much he couldn't grab it. The whips carried on beating her. At last he grabbed the whistle and blew. The whips stopped.

"Into the whistle," ordered the old man. In a moment they were gone. The old woman kissed her husband and promised never to scold again.

"Let's eat, shall we?" said the old man. They sat down to a fine spread and not a cross word was said and they went to bed the best of friends.

By the next morning, the old woman had forgotten her promises. She told him off for staying in bed so long, then she sent him up the tower to check on the turnips.

He came down smiling. "They're fine," he said. "None of them have been touched."

"I don't believe you," shouted the old woman. She tried to climb the stairs, but they were too narrow and twisty. She grew angrier and angrier.

"You'll have to carry me!" she ordered.

"But how?" asked the old man. "I need both hands to climb the ladder."

"I'll get into the flour sack and you can carry me up in that with your teeth." And she got into the sack.

The old man picked her up, held the sack in his teeth and started to climb. But it was a long way and a very slow climb.

"Are we at the top?" asked the old woman from inside the sack.

The old man kept climbing, not saying a word.

"Are we near the top?" she screamed again.

The old man kept climbing.

The old woman jumped around in the sack. "Answer me, you fool! Are we at the top yet?" she raged.

"Almost," said the old man.

But, as he opened his mouth, the sack, with its contents, tumbled down the stairs to the ground.

And that was the end of the old woman.

The old man lived on alone in the cottage. He was quite happy. He had his tablecloth for his meals, he had the goat that sneezed gold for whenever he needed to buy anything in the village and he had his whistle to drive away any unwanted visitors. But when he wanted company, he would go to the clearing in the woods and play with the little children in the hut and he would often take them turnips as they enjoyed them so much.

Beauty and the Beast

Once upon a time there was a rich merchant. He lived with his family in a fine house in the middle of a prosperous city by the sea. He had three daughters, all beautiful girls but the youngest was the prettiest of them all and she was called Beauty.

One day the merchant received terrible news. All his ships had sunk in a storm and he had lost all his money. He had to sell his fine house and his daughters had to sell their jewellery. They all moved to a tiny cottage in a village away from the city.

They had very little money left, just enough to buy food. They could not afford to have servants now. Instead it was Beauty who did the work.

She was very happy to help her father, so she cooked and cleaned and tended the vegetable and herb gardens. Her sisters did nothing to help. They sat and lazed all day, thinking about when they had been rich.

One day a messenger came from the city.

"I have good news for you, merchant," he said. "Not all your ships were lost in the storm. One struggled into harbour just a day ago with its cargo intact. I came with all speed to tell you."

The merchant was delighted. And so were his daughters.

"Does it mean we can move back to the city?" asked the oldest sister.

"Can we buy all our jewels back?" asked the middle sister.

"We shall see, we shall see," said the merchant and he prepared to leave for the city. When he was ready he asked his daughters what they would like him to bring back for them.

"A ruby necklace," said the first.

"A pearl bracelet," said the second.

"Father, I will be happy if you bring me a rose," said Beauty.

The merchant went to the city and saw his lawyers. He sold the cargo and completed his business. When he had finished, he went to buy the presents for his daughters. He found the ruby necklace and the pearl bracelet but he could not find a rose for Beauty. He searched for so long that he was late leaving the city. When night fell, he was still far from home, in the middle of a dark wood. He decided he would find somewhere to stay for the night.

After an hour or so of wandering, he spotted some lights in the distance. He made his way to them and found himself outside a large mansion.

"I must be lost," the merchant said to himself. "Because I've certainly never seen this house before."

As he stood there, the door opened and because he was tired and hungry, the merchant went in. The door closed behind him, but there was no one there.

Suddenly he could smell food. The door in front of him opened showing a room already prepared. A fire was burning in the hearth and candles were glowing. The table was set for one person with lots of delicious food set around. He sat down and ate his fill. When he had finished he thanked his unseen host.

Still he had seen no one, not a footman or a maid. He made his way upstairs to find a room prepared. The lamp was glowing and a fire burned in the grate.

"This is very strange," said the merchant as he settled down to sleep.

In the morning when he awoke he found his clothes all freshly laundered, his breakfast was ready and when he went outside he found his horse had been stabled and fed.

Then he saw the rose garden. There, beside the house were the most beautiful roses in all shades of pink and red, orange and yellow. The merchant was delighted.

"Now I can get Beauty's present," he said. He reached up to pick one of the reddest roses he could see. Just as the stem broke, there was a terrible roar behind him. The merchant nearly leapt out of his skin and almost dropped the rose, but he turned round to see what was there.

In front of him stood the most frightening creature he had ever seen. It had the body of a man and the head of a beast.

"I have given you free run of my home," roared the Beast. "You have eaten at my table, slept in my bed and you repay me by stealing from my garden!"

"I did not mean to steal," said the merchant, shaking. "I was picking the rose for my youngest daughter. She asked me for a rose as her present. I'm sorry. I didn't realise."

"If you do not wish to die," said the Beast, "you must return here in three day's time bringing with you the first living thing that greets you when you arrive home."

"I shall do as you say," said the merchant, realising with relief that his dog was always the first to greet him.

"You may take the rose and go," said the Beast and he turned away. The merchant shuddered at the sight of him. He then collected his horse and belongings and left the mansion.

As the merchant rode up to the cottage, the dog was lying fast asleep in the sun. It was Beauty, not the dog, who ran out to greet her father.

"Oh, Beauty," said the merchant, sadly. "Not you."

"What is it, father?" asked Beauty. "What's the matter?"

Just then, the two other sisters ran out of the house.

"Did you bring my necklace?" asked the first.

"Have you got my bracelet?" asked the other.

"Yes," said their father. "They are in the saddlebags." He went into the cottage with Beauty, leaving the two sisters fighting to open the bags.

"Please tell me what's wrong," begged Beauty.

"I must leave you in three days and I will not return," said the merchant.

"Why?" asked Beauty. "What has happened?"

At first the merchant would not tell his daughter what had happened at the Beast's mansion. But she pleaded so much that he finally told her.

"I will go to him, father," said Beauty quietly. "I won't let him kill you."

The merchant was very upset but he could not persuade Beauty against going to the Beast.

Two days later, Beauty and her father left for the Beast's mansion. They said farewell at the gate and Beauty went up to the house alone. The door opened and she went inside.

Beauty heard the door close behind her but saw no one. She wandered from room to room looking for someone to talk to, but there was no one there. The house was beautifully furnished, rich carpets lay on the floors and fine pictures hung on the walls.

For the first few days, Beauty was alone. She was free to wander around the house – no doors were locked to her. Still she saw no one, and yet she had everything she needed. One day embroidery threads were waiting for her, another day books arrived so that she wouldn't be bored. She had things to do but she longed for someone to talk to.

One day she was doing her embroidery by the window, when she heard a voice behind her.

"Don't be frightened," he said. "I will not hurt you. You may turn around

and look at me. I'm sorry I am so ugly but please believe that I will not harm you."

Beauty turned round and came face to face with the Beast. Her father had told her how ugly he was, but she still shuddered when she saw him. His eyes looked away, avoiding hers, and Beauty was immediately sorry.

"You are free to go where you like in the grounds and in the house," said the Beast. "But please don't go out of the gates."

The days passed and the Beast would spend part of the day with Beauty. Gradually she became used to him and even looked forward to seeing him for she was lonely and very homesick. The Beast saw this and one day he gave her a mirror.

"When you look into it," he said, "you will see whoever you wish to see."

"Does that mean I can see my father?" asked Beauty eagerly.

"Yes, it does," said the Beast and he left her alone with the mirror.

Beauty looked and saw the cottage and then she saw her father and sisters. Her father looked sad, and tears came to Beauty's eyes, but her sisters looked happy. They were obviously preparing for a wedding. Beauty ran off to find the Beast.

"Please, may I go home for a few days?" she asked. "My sister is getting married and I would like to be there. May I go?"

"Yes," said the Beast. "You may have one week. Please be back here on the evening of the seventh day. You will find clothes packed and the carriage will be ready. Goodbye."

He turned away leaving Beauty alone. When she saw the clothes that had been prepared, she couldn't believe the richness of the colours and fabrics. The carriage soon took her home and she was reunited with her father and sisters.

The wedding took place amid great celebration and the sister went to live with her new husband in the city. At the end of the week Beauty prepared to go back to the Beast.

"You don't have to go there," said her father. "We must be able to do something."

"I must go," replied Beauty. "I promised. Besides, I'm well cared for, I want for nothing."

So Beauty returned to the Beast. Life continued as before. The Beast would spend part of the day with her. One day he asked her a question.

"Beauty," he said. "Do you love me?"

"Love you?" repeated Beauty. "No, I don't love you. I like you. I'm not afraid of you. But I don't love you."

"Ah, well," sighed the Beast and he left Beauty alone for the day.

Once a week, Beauty would look in her mirror to see her family. One day she noticed that there were again preparations for a wedding.

"Please, may I go?" she asked the Beast. "My other sister is marrying. I promise I shall return in a week."

The Beast gave his permission and Beauty left and joined her family for the wedding. It was a very happy occasion. Her father was overjoyed to have Beauty back. But at the end of the week Beauty prepared to return to the Beast. Her father again tried to persuade her to stay.

"I promised, father," she said. "I have to go."

Beauty returned to the Beast's mansion, where she was welcomed gladly. He gave her many gifts over the next few days. Beauty was touched and realised that the Beast had missed her.

The summer days passed and the Beast spent most of the day and most evenings with Beauty. She looked forward to their time together and missed his company when he was not there. After a while she forgot to use the mirror to see her family.

One day she remembered and looked quickly into the mirror. What she saw made the blood drain from her face. Her father was lying ill in bed. He was calling out Beauty's name.

She ran to the Beast, tears running down her face. "My father is ill," she wept. "He looks as though he's dying. Please can I go to him?"

"Of course, but you must promise to return," said the Beast. "Take this with you." He gave her a pearl ring. "If the stone grows dull, you will know I am ill. If it turns black, you will know I am dying. Please wear it all the time."

Beauty took the ring and put it on her finger and left for her father's cottage. When she arrived, she found her sisters there.

"At last," they cried. "Where have you been? He's been asking for you. Now you're here he might recover."

As soon as he saw Beauty, the merchant felt better. Beauty stayed and nursed him and the weeks passed. He gradually grew stronger and then winter came.

"Stay here for winter," said her father. "I'm sure the Beast would not expect you to travel in this weather."

So Beauty stayed on and by spring the merchant was almost back to full health.

"Stay for spring," he told Beauty. "Stay until I'm completely recovered." So Beauty stayed until the flowers were blooming. One day Beauty was tidying some drawers when she found the ring the Beast had given her. She had looked at it every day for the first few weeks and seen no change. Then she had put it away for safety and forgotten all about it.

This time the pearl on the ring was totally black. "Oh no," cried Beauty. "Oh, Beast! What have I done?"

She rushed to her father. "I must go," she cried. "The Beast needs me. He's dying. He may already be dead!"

With that she ran from the cottage and the carriage took her to the Beast's mansion. She ran into the mansion but could find no sign of the Beast. She called out for him, but there was no answer. Then she ran into the gardens still calling for him.

She heard a sigh come from the rose bushes nearby. There, on the ground, lay the Beast. Beauty ran up to him and knelt down. Tears were pouring down her face as she cradled his ugly head in her arms.

"Oh, Beast," she cried. "I'm sorry. I didn't mean to leave you alone for so long." The Beast lay unmoving in her arms and she wept harder.

"Please don't die," she begged. "You're too good and kind and I don't want to lose you. I promise I'll stay here and I'll never leave you. I love you, Beast."

With her final words, the earth seemed to shake and shudder and Beauty found that she was sitting by the rose bush alone. There was no sign of the Beast.

"Beauty," said a voice behind her. It sounded like the Beast's.

Beauty turned round and standing before her was a handsome young man. She looked around for the Beast.

"Where's the Beast?" she asked.

"I am the Beast," replied the young man. "I was under a spell by my stepmother. She turned me into a Beast as punishment for something I did not do. The spell could only be broken by someone saying that she loved me. I was so ugly, I thought I was doomed to live out my life as a beast, but you have broken the spell."

Beauty was overjoyed and she and the young man were married soon after. Her father and sisters were all invited to the Beast's mansion for the wedding which was celebrated with the scent of rose blossom filling the air.

The Godson of the French King

There once lived a poor man in the middle of the forest. He already had twenty-five sons, and one day his twenty-sixth son was born. Now when a man has twenty-six children it is very hard to find yet another godfather.

The poor man had asked all his neighbours, but they all said no. Some of them were already godfathers three times over! So the poor man set out into the world to find a godfather for his youngest son.

He was very lucky. As he left the forest, he saw riding along the road, the King of France's carriage. The man bowed to the King.

The French King threw out a gold coin. "Here is a souvenir," he said.

"Thank you, my lord, a gold coin is always useful but I need something other than gold."

"What do you need?" asked the King.

"I have twenty-five children, all boys, and my twenty-sixth child, another son, has just been born. I am looking for a godfather for him."

"Twenty-six sons!" said the amazed King. "I can see your problem. In that case, I shall be his godfather."

"Thank you, your majesty," said the poor man. "Thank you very much."

The next day the French King came to the baby boy's christening and stood as godfather and the baby was christened Louis, after the King. Before the King left, he gave a bag of gold to the man.

"When he is seven, send him to school for his education. And when he is eighteen, give him this and send him to my court," and he gave the poor man half of his royal ring. "He shall be well looked after."

The boy grew up and when he was seven he started school. He was a good scholar and learnt well. When he was eighteen, his father gave him the half ring and said: "Take this ring to your godfather, the French King. He will see that you are well looked after. But remember us, your father and your twenty-five brothers."

Louis went on his way with the ring wrapped in a scarf in his pocket. His father had given him an old horse so that he would not arrive on foot. Some way along the road he met an old man, who was walking. He looked as though he could hardly take another step. Louis jumped down from his horse.

"Good day, old man," he said. "Would you care to ride?"

"Thank you, godson of the French King," said the old man. "I will."

The boy was most surprised that the old man knew who he was. They travelled for a few more hours, with the old man riding the horse.

They came to a fork in the road and the old man dismounted.

"Thank you, my lad," said the old man. "A small piece of advice. Beware of strangers and don't go near water with people you don't know. Not even a well." And the old man took one fork of the road while Louis took the other going to Paris.

He had not gone more than a mile, when he heard someone calling him. A young man was following him down the road.

"Hello, Louis, godson of the French King," the young man called. "Wait for me!"

Louis was surprised because he did not know the man, but he slowed down, forgetting the old man's warning.

"Do you remember me?" asked the man. "We were at school together."

Louis could not remember, but felt that they must have been if the young man remembered.

"I'm going to Paris," said Louis. "So I must keep going."

"So am I," said the young man. "Let's ride together."

They rode on a little way until they came to the forest.

"Let's stop for a drink," said the young man. "There's a well just here."

"No, I can't," said Louis, remembering the old man's warning just in time. "I have to go on."

"A rest will do the horses good," said the young man and he led the horses off the road. They reached the well where the young man knelt and drank. "Have a drink," he called to Louis.

Louis leaned over the well to drink, and the stranger pushed him head first into the well. "Now the ring is mine," said the stranger as he grabbed the scarf holding the ring. He then went on his way to Paris.

Luckily, Louis did not drown. He pulled himself out of the well, leapt on his horse and galloped after the stranger. But the young man beat him to the city gate.

"Give me back my ring," Louis shouted to the thief.

"What ring?" said the young man. "This ring belongs to the godson of the French King. I am his godson, the ring is mine. One more word and I shall have the King lock you up. But if you're sensible I'll ask the King to give you a job, looking after horses."

Louis could do nothing. He bit his tongue and bided his time.

The false godson went straight to the King.

"Here is your half ring, French King," said the young man. "I am your godson."

Now the King did not particularly like the look of this young man. He was not at all the way he had imagined. The young boy next to him looked much more the way he expected.

"Who is that with you?" asked the King, pointing to Louis.

"Just a lad from the village," said the young man. "He came along to see Paris and to serve the King but really he would be happiest cleaning out the stables!"

So Louis was sent to work in the stables, while the false godson went everywhere with the King. The King had no children, so there was the possibility that he would name his godson as his heir.

The false godson continually thought of Louis and decided that he would have to get rid of him. He went to the King one day.

"Did you know, Godfather, that your new stable lad has been boasting he would ask the sun why it is red in the morning," said the false godson.

"That would be interesting to know," said the French King, thoughtfully. "He can go and find out tomorrow. Bring the lad here."

So Louis was brought before the King.

"I hear you're boasting you can ask the sun why it's red in the morning," said the King.

"That's a lie, sire," said Louis. "I said no such thing."

But the King would not hear another word and he sent Louis to find out why the sun was so red. Sadly, Louis got on his horse, and went on his way.

After a while he met an old man. It was the same old man he had met on his way to Paris.

"Where are you going, godson of the French King?" the old man asked.

"To the sun, old man," said Louis, sadly.

"If you had listened to me, you wouldn't be here now," said the old man. "But never mind. Get on this wooden horse and it will take you to the glass mountain." He led a wooden horse out from behind a tree. "Your horse would never get you there."

"Thank you old man," cried Louis and he leapt onto the wooden horse, which spread wings and rose high into the sky. It flew over the sea and landed at the foot of the glass mountain.

It took Louis all day to climb to the castle at the top. The castle was made of pure gold and nearly blinded him. He knocked loudly at the gate.

An old woman came to the door. She was the sun's mother. "What do you want, godson of the French King?"

"Is the sun at home?" asked Louis.

"He's not," said the old woman. "But he will be back soon."

"May I wait?" asked Louis.

"Of course," replied the old woman. "But he will be hungry, so I shall hide you until he's eaten." She hid him in a cupboard.

The next moment there was a tremendous roar as the sun walked into the kitchen. After he had eaten, his mother told Louis to come out.

"Good evening, sun," said Louis. "I have come to ask you why you are a beautiful red colour in the morning."

"Good evening, godson of the French King," said the sun. "It is because I rise beside the castle of the Princess of Tronkolen. She is so beautiful she almost outshines me, so I have to appear at my best."

"Thank you, sun. Thank you, old woman," said Louis. He said goodbye and then went back down the hill to the wooden horse. The horse carried him across the sea back to the old man.

"How did you get on, godson of the French King?" asked the old man.

"The sun told me what I wanted to know. Thank you for your help."

"Not at all," said the old man and he went on his way.

Next morning, Louis went to the French King.

"You're back quickly. Do you have an answer?" said the King.

"Yes. The sun rises beside the castle of Tronkolen, where the Princess lives. She is so beautiful that the sun always has to appear at his best!"

The French King was happy with the answer and he gave Louis a bag of gold. The false godson was not at all happy. He began to think of other ways of getting rid of Louis.

Then he had an idea. He went to the King. "Godfather," he said, "your new stable lad is boasting again."

"What is he saying this time?"

"That he will go to fetch the Princess of Tronkolen, and marry her," lied the false godson.

"He will not," cried the King. "I shall have her for my wife. Bring the stable lad to me."

Louis was brought before the King and again denied he had said anything about the Princess of Tronkolen.

"You must fetch her tomorrow, or I'll have your head cut off," said the French King.

Poor Louis set off again for the east. A little way out of town, he met the old man again.

"Where are you going, godson of the French King?" he asked.

"To the island of Tronkolen. The French King wants to marry the Princess," replied Louis.

"Return to the French King and ask him for a ship, with a load of wheat, bacon and beef. You will need these to fetch the Princess."

Louis returned and told the King, who immediately provided a ship with its load of beef, bacon and wheat. When it was ready to sail the old man appeared and gave Louis a white stick.

"This stick will lead you. You will first come to an island of ants. The wheat is for them. Next you will come to an island of lions, give them the bacon. Finally you will reach the island of hawks. The beef is for them. The way to the island of Tronkolen will then be clear, but be warned, Louis, be careful that the Princess of Tronkolen does not see you before you see her. If not she will put a spell on you. Good luck!"

"Thank you, old man," said Louis, as he pointed the white stick. The ship sped off, leaving the port far behind. They soon reached the island of ants, where Louis gave them the wheat.

"If ever you need help, godson of the French King, just think of us and we'll be there," said the King of the Ants.

The second island was bigger than the first. It was the island of lions and Louis gave the bacon to the King of the lions.

"If ever you need help, just think of us and we'll be there," said the King.

The next island was even bigger than the other two. It was the island of hawks. Louis gave them the beef.

"If ever you need help, think of us and we'll be there," said the King of the Hawks.

Louis left the island, and the ship shot forward. In a moment or two another island appeared. Louis could see a shining crystal castle. He landed and went ashore. Around the castle was a beautiful garden.

Louis climbed an orange tree and waited. Eventually a young girl walked into the garden. She was the most beautiful girl he had ever seen. She combed out her long golden hair and used the surface of the well as a mirror. Louis looked for a long time and then dropped an orange to break the reflection.

She looked up. "Is that you, Louis, godson of the French King?" she asked. "Come down and we'll go to the castle."

The next two weeks flew by as Louis and the Princess got to know each other. Then Louis remembered why he had come.

"Will you come back with me to the French King?" he asked.

"Gladly," said the Princess, "but first you must prove yourself worthy. You must perform three tasks."

The next day, the Princess took him to a huge pile of grain. "You must sort this into the four types," she told him. "You have until sunset."

By midday, Louis had hardly sorted out a handful of each. "I must get help," he said to himself, then he remembered the ants. No sooner had he thought of them, than they were there.

"How can we help, godson of the French King," they asked.

Louis told them his task. The ants set to work and a few moments later the grain was sorted into four piles, not a single grain in the wrong pile. So Louis lay down and went to sleep.

When the sun was setting, the Princess returned. She was delighted. She kissed Louis on the forehead. The next day, she gave him the second task. She led him to an oak forest.

"Do you see these old oak trees?" she said. "They must be cut down by sunset."

Louis set to work, but by midday, he was just starting the second tree.

'I need help,' he thought. 'I shall call on the lions.' The lions arrived an instant later.

"How can we help?" they asked.

"Help me cut down these oak trees," he said. The lions set to and a moment later all the trees were cut down. Louis lay down and went to sleep.

At sunset the Princess returned. She was amazed and delighted that the task was completed. She kissed Louis twice on the forehead.

The next day, the Princess gave him the third and most difficult task. She took Louis to the other side of the castle.

"Do you see this mountain? It casts too big a shadow over the castle and garden. Your third task is to level it."

Louis set to and filled a wheelbarrow and dumped the earth in the sea. By midday he had done this four times.

'I need help,' he thought. 'Maybe the hawks can help.' The hawks appeared a moment later.

"How can we help, godson of the French King?" they asked.

"Help me to level this mountain," said Louis. The hawks set to and in no time at all, the mountain was levelled. Louis lay down and went to sleep.

The Princess returned at sunset to find the third task completed.

"I shall marry only Louis," she said as she kissed him three times on the forehead.

Louis woke up. "Are you happy, Princess?" he asked. "Will you come away with me?"

"I will go wherever you say, Louis," said the Princess.

"We shall go to my godfather, the French King," said Louis and he led the way to his ship. There he raised the white stick and the ship leapt forward and in no time they were back at the port.

The old man was waiting for them. "Welcome, Princess of Tronkolen, soon to be married. Welcome, Louis, godson of the French King, soon to be the heir of the King."

"Thank you, old man," said Louis. "I could never have done this without you."

When they reached the King's castle, the French King could hardly take his eyes off the Princess. He thought her the most beautiful girl he had ever seen. He was delighted that she was to be his wife.

The false godson was green with envy. He tried for days to think of some way to get rid of Louis. Then he had an idea.

One day he said to the French King, "Have you heard that the stable boy says he will marry the Princess?"

"He will not," said the King. "Bring him here. The Princess shall be my bride."

Louis was brought before the King. With him was the Princess.

The King stood up there and then and asked the Princess to be his wife.

The Princess laughed: "Thank you, French King! But you're old enough to be my grandfather. I shall marry a younger man."

"If that is the case," said the King, "then marry my godson, here."
He pointed to the false godson.

The Princess laughed again. "I will gladly marry your godson, French King, but not that liar and traitor. Your real godson is standing next to me." And she took Louis' hand.

The false godson went pink, then scarlet. Anyone looking at him would know that he had been lying all along.

"Where did you get my half ring?" roared the King.

"He stole it from me," said Louis. He told the King the whole story.

The King was furious. "Take that man out and behead him!" he ordered the guards.

A few days later, the Princess of Tronkolen and Louis, the godson of the French King, were married. At the feast Louis did not forget who had helped him. At the King's table sat the old man, the Kings of Ants, Lions and Hawks, Louis' father and his twenty-five brothers.

All lived happily ever after.

The Caliph Turned Stork

Chasid, the Caliph of Baghdad, liked to spend part of his afternoon relaxing. Affairs of state were carried out in the morning, but after lunch he always insisted on time to think about the day's events. He would lay back on his divan drinking coffee, and feel thoroughly at peace with the world. This was always a good time to talk to Chasid, which was why Mansor, the Grand Vizier, tended to choose this time of the day to visit.

Mansor arrived one particular afternoon, looking very thoughtful.

"Why so serious, Grand Vizier?" asked the Caliph from his divan.

The Grand Vizier bowed low before the Caliph. "I didn't realise I was looking serious, sire. But I was thinking about a pedlar who is in the courtyard. He has such marvellous things for sale, and at a time when I have no spare money to buy any of them."

The Caliph had wanted for some time to buy something special for his Grand Vizier and he realised that here was the opportunity. The pedlar was sent for and he spread out his wares before the Caliph. There were rings, bracelets, goblets, pistols, combs and many other things. The Caliph eventually decided on a pair of pistols for himself and the same for the Vizier. He also bought a comb for Mansor's wife.

As the pedlar was putting away his wares, the Caliph noticed a small drawer.

"Is there anything in there which might be for sale?" he asked the pedlar.

The pedlar took out a small gold box and a piece of parchment with some writing on it. In the box was some powder. Neither the Caliph nor his Grand Vizier could read what was written on the parchment.

The pedlar told them, "I was given these by a merchant who found them in a street in Mecca. I don't know if they are of value, but you can have them for a small sum. They are of no use to me."

The Caliph, who collected old manuscripts, gladly bought the box and the parchment. After the pedlar had gone, the Caliph turned to the Grand Vizier. "I want to know what is written here, Mansor," he said. "How can I find out?"

"Well, sire," said the Grand Vizier. "I have heard there is a wise man in the city who can read all languages. His name is Selim. Maybe he can read it for us."

Selim was brought before the Caliph.

"Selim," said the Caliph, "I have heard it said that you are a wise man. Look at this manuscript and see if you can read it. If you can understand it and tell us its meaning, you will be handsomely rewarded."

Selim looked closely at the writing and then cried, "It is Latin, my lord! I swear it is in Latin."

"Tell us what it means," commanded the Caliph.

So Selim translated for them. "'Whoever takes a pinch of the powder and puts it to his nostrils and calls out the word *mutabor*, can change at will to any animal and will understand the language of all animals. To regain his former shape he must bow three times towards the east, saying the same word – *mutabor*. But take great care that while in the animal form he does not laugh, for if he does the word will go forever from his memory. He will be doomed to remain a beast.'"

The Caliph was delighted. Selim was sworn to secrecy and rewarded.

"This is a marvellous thing," said the Caliph to the Grand Vizier. "Tomorrow morning we will put it to the test."

Early the next day the Grand Vizier arrived. The Caliph put the gold box in a pocket and off they went. They strolled down to the meadows.

"There is a pond, sire," suggested the Grand Vizier. "Storks are frequent visitors there."

"Come then," said the Caliph. "We shall see the storks."

At the pond, they found a stork pacing up and down looking for frogs. Another was flying down to join it.

"Do you not think, sire," said the Grand Vizier, "that they will hold an interesting conversation?"

"Let's turn into storks and listen to it," said the Caliph. "And to turn back remember, we must bow three times to the east and say *mutabor*. But, remember, we must not laugh at any time. Come."

He took a pinch of the powder and offered the box to the Grand Vizier who also took a pinch. They held the powder to their noses and said the magic word, "*Mutabor!*"

Instantly, their legs shrank to long red sticks, their noses grew into beaks, their necks grew and grew, feathers started appearing and instead of beautiful slippers, they had clumsy storks' feet.

"What a beautiful beak you have, Grand Vizier," said the Caliph. "This really is amazing!"

"I must say, sire, you are by far the handsomest stork I have ever seen," said the Grand Vizier. Then he looked at the other storks. "I wonder what they are saying."

By this time the other stork had landed. The Caliph and the Grand Vizier moved closer.

"Good morning, Madame Longshanks," called the new arrival.

"Good morning to you, Mistress Clatterbill," said the other. "Would you care to join me in some breakfast?"

"I really think I am too nervous to eat. I have to dance for my father and his guests tonight. I came here to practise." With that she started hopping, skipping and flapping about. She hopped from one foot to another, throwing her wings out to stop herself falling over, all the while stretching her neck out. But when she tried to pirouette on one toe, it was too much for the Caliph and the Grand Vizier. They roared with laughter and could not stop. Tears rolled down their feathered cheeks.

Then the Grand Vizier suddenly remembered the warning. He told the Caliph.

"I can't stay a bird all my life!" cried the Caliph. "What was the word to change us back? I can't remember it!"

"We bow three times to the east and say mu-mu-mu-mu," said the Grand Vizier unable to remember the word either.

They tried but the word would not come back to them. They wandered sadly away. How could they go back to the city and say their Caliph was a stork? Who would believe them and who would want to be ruled by a stork?

They wandered around for several days, trying to learn to eat fruit and berries with their new beaks. They did not like the idea of eating newts or frogs legs!

They could fly though, which they did frequently, and one afternoon they flew over Baghdad. Far below they saw a procession, drums were beating and the crowds were calling, "Hail Mizra! Hail Mizra! Ruler of Baghdad!"

"Do you hear that, Mansor?" said Chasid, indignantly. "Now we know who is behind our enchantment. Mizra is the son of my greatest enemy, the magician Kaschnur. He swore vengeance and now he has it. Come, we shall fly to Mohammed's tomb. Surely in that holy place, we shall be transformed back to our rightful shapes."

The two storks flew from the roof of the palace off in the direction of Medina. After some time, the Grand Vizier groaned, "Please, my lord, may we not stop to rest. It is nearly night and I cannot go on much longer."

Below them were the ruins of a palace. They landed in a courtyard and headed for a corridor. Mansor suddenly stopped. "There are ghosts! What is that weeping and wailing?" he cried.

Chasid heard the weeping and headed in that direction.

"My lord," called the Grand Vizier after him, "it may be dangerous."

Chasid ignored him and continued down the corridor. At the end was a room with the door slightly open. The sound of weeping came from the room. Mansor scurried after the Caliph.

Chasid pushed the door open with his beak and they could see a dark, dismal room. The setting sun gave a little light through a grating. There on the floor sat a large owl. Tears fell from its great round eyes as it sat weeping. It heard the door open and saw the two storks.

Its face lit up as it spoke to them in a human voice. "Oh, welcome, storks! Now I know I will be saved. The prophecy was right!"

When Chasid had got over his surprise, he said, "My dear owl, from what you say, we are all under some enchantment. But I'm afraid I cannot see how we can help."

He then told the owl what had happened to them.

"It was the same magician who did this to me," said the owl. "My name is Lusa. My father is an Indian Prince. He refused to marry me to the magician's son, Mizra. So Kaschnur turned me into an owl and imprisoned me in this room. He told me I would stay this way until someone chooses me as his bride. I have been here many months. He made life as difficult for me as he could, for I am blind by day. I can see only at night."

The Caliph listened carefully. "It would seem our enchantments are somehow linked. But we must find a way to break the spells."

"There is definitely a link," said the owl. "When I was a child, a wise woman prophesied that a stork would bring me great joy and fortune. I do have an idea how we can save ourselves."

"How?" said the Caliph.

"Kaschnur comes here once a month and meets with his friends, other magicians. They boast of their latest magic. Maybe he will tell your story at the next meeting and repeat the magic word."

"When does he visit?" asked Chasid, excitedly. "Where will they meet?"

"Please do not be angry, but I will tell you on one condition," said the owl.

"I do not want to stay like this for the rest of my life. The spell can only be broken if one of you offers his hand in marriage."

The two storks looked at each other. Then the Caliph and his Grand Vizier went out into the corridor.

"Of course," said the Caliph, "you'll marry her, won't you."

"I would be delighted to serve, sire," said the Grand Vizier. "But I dread to think what my wife would say! Besides I am old. You are young and unmarried. You are in a much better position to make a young and beautiful princess your wife."

"Ah, but that's it," said Chasid. "How do we know she's young and beautiful. It could be very tricky."

They argued back and forth for several minutes, but finally the Caliph saw that Mansor would rather stay as a stork than marry an owl.

"Very well," said Chasid. "I shall marry her."

The owl was overjoyed by their decision. "The meeting of the magicians will take place tonight in the great hall at the other end of the palace. I'll show you the way."

She flew ahead and stopped beside a wall. "I often listen here," she said, "hoping to hear something that might help me."

There was a small hole in the wall and they could see into the room beyond. The room was richly decorated with tapestries and carpets. The table was set with fine food and eight men were seated at the table. The Caliph instantly recognised one as the pedlar who had sold him the powder. After a while it was his turn to tell the tale of his latest enchantments.

"I have enchanted the Caliph of Baghdad and his Grand Vizier," he boasted. "My son now sits on the throne." The other magicians were very impressed. One asked how it had been done.

"I sold him a magic powder and gave him a magic word on parchment," said Kaschnur.

"What was the word?" asked one.

The two storks listened with bated breath for the next few words.

"Oh, it was a difficult one, a Latin word," said Kaschnur. "It was *mutabor*."

Chasid and Mansor were delighted. They raced down the corridors and out of the ruined palace. When they were outside, the Caliph turned to the owl. "Oh, fair one," he said. "Please take me as your husband. Be my wife to the end of our days."

Then he turned to the east with the Grand Vizier. Together they bowed three times and said *"Mutabor!"* just as the sun was rising above the horizon.

They were instantly turned back to their former selves. They fell into each others arms in their joy.

Then they looked around for their companion. Before them stood the most beautiful girl either man had ever seen. She laughed as she held her hand out to the surprised Caliph. "Yes," she said. "I am your friend the owl."

The Caliph was enchanted and said, "I do believe that being changed into a stork is the best thing that has ever happened to me! If I hadn't, I would never have met you, Lusa."

They immediately set out for Baghdad. When they arrived the people were overjoyed to see them again. Mizra was not a popular ruler and when the Caliph arrived the people rushed to the palace and grabbed Mizra and his father. Kaschnur the magician, was condemned to hang in the room where the owl had been imprisoned. Mizra was given the choice of death or a pinch of the magic powder. He chose the powder and ended his days as a stork in a great iron cage in the palace garden.

The Caliph and Lusa were married and spent many happy years together. Their favourite times were when the Grand Vizier came on his daily visit during the afternoon. They would often talk of their 'stork days' together.

Needless to say, the Grand Vizier never again invited pedlars into the palace to sell their wares.

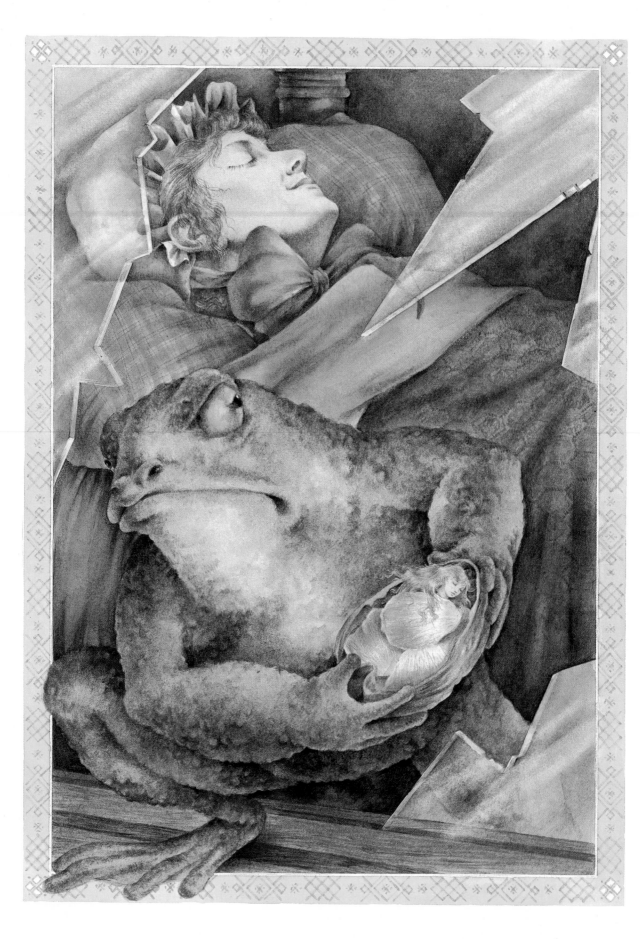

Thumbelina

There was once a woman who longed for a child. She went to ask an old witch how she could get one.

"I wish I could have a child," she told the witch. "I wouldn't mind if she were as small as my thumb. Can you help me?"

"Certainly," said the witch. "Here is a barley seed. It's not an ordinary seed though. Plant it in a flower pot and you shall see what you shall see."

The woman thanked the witch and went home to plant the seed. Within a day a beautiful flower had grown. It looked just like a tulip.

As the woman bent over to have a closer look, the flower opened and there, in the centre of the flower stood a tiny girl. She was delicate and beautiful and hardly the length of the woman's thumb. She was called Thumbelina.

Thumbelina had a half walnut shell for her bed, violet petals were her mattress and rose petals were the covers. Her days were spent playing. Her mother filled a plate with water and put flowers around it, then Thumbelina would sit on a rose leaf and row herself across.

One night, while Thumbelina and her mother were fast asleep, a toad crept in through a broken window pane. She had seen Thumbelina several times and had decided that she would be the perfect wife for her son.

"Beautiful," muttered the old toad as she picked up Thumbelina's walnut-shell bed. "You are the ideal wife for my son," she croaked.

She hopped away with Thumbelina still asleep in her bed. The toad took her down to the brook that ran by the house and then fetched her son.

"Here is your wife, my son," said the old toad.

"Grook, grook," was all the young toad could say.

"Don't speak so loudly, or you'll wake her," said his mother. "Now go and prepare the marriage home for her, while I put her somewhere safe."

The young toad disappeared into the soggy mud to prepare rooms for Thumbelina under the marsh. His mother took the walnut-shell with the sleeping girl into the middle of the brook and placed her on a wide lily leaf.

As dawn broke, Thumbelina awoke to find herself trapped in the middle of the brook. She was so scared, she started to cry. There was no way for her to reach land.

The old toad and her son were busy preparing Thumbelina's room. Then in the middle of the morning they swam out to the leaf. They wanted to take the bed down to the bridal chamber.

The old toad bowed low in the water. "This is my son," she said. "He will be your husband and you will live happily together in the marsh." With that, she took Thumbelina's walnut bed and swam away with it.

Thumbelina was left alone on the leaf, crying. The fish in the brook came up to take a look at her. They took pity on her, because she was so pretty and decided to save her from marrying the toad. They bit through the stalk holding the leaf and let the leaf run downstream with the brook, taking her far from home.

Thumbelina sailed past many cities, leaving the toads far behind her. The birds in the bushes would sing to her as she sailed by. A great white butterfly flew with her for several days. He told her of the places they were passing. She eventually tied her belt to the butterfly so that the butterfly could drag the leaf even faster through the water.

One day, a blackbird saw her and thought her the prettiest thing he had ever seen. He flew down and plucked Thumbelina off the leaf. The leaf sailed on downstream with the butterfly still pulling it.

Thumbelina was terrified when the bird flew off with her into a tree but she was more worried about the butterfly who was still tied to the leaf. The blackbird was not worried about this at all and he landed in the tree and put Thumbelina on a branch. The other blackbirds gathered around.

"She's very skinny," said one.

"She has no feelers," said another. "She can't be good to eat."

"She looks just like a small human," said a third. "I think she's ugly!"

"Well, I think she's pretty," said the blackbird who had picked her up. Poor Thumbelina sat and listened to the arguments.

"She's not pretty," said one of the other birds and the others agreed with him. Slowly they convinced the blackbird that Thumbelina was ugly and that he should have nothing more to do with her.

"You're right," he said at last. "She's ugly." And he picked her up and took her down to the ground. He put her on a daisy and left her there.

Thumbelina wept. "I'm so ugly!" she cried. "No one will talk to me!"

Poor Thumbelina lived alone in the woods for the whole summer. She wove a mat out of grass to sleep on and she tied it underneath a flower for shelter. She ate the honey from the flowers and drank the dew on the leaves in the morning. Autumn came and many of the birds flew away.

The flowers started to shrivel and die and Thumbelina was left with no shelter when the rains came. Her dress was shabby and torn, so she wrapped herself in a dry leaf but that cracked and let in the cold.

She grew colder and hungrier. Winter came and the snow started to fall, but the snow flakes were so large to little Thumbelina that they almost knocked her over.

Close to the wood there was a cornfield. The corn had been cut many weeks before, when the weather had still been warm. Now all that was left was stubble. Thumbelina was making her way along the edge of the cornfield looking for shelter, when she came upon a field mouse's front door. She knocked and the field mouse came to the door.

"Please can you spare me a little corn?" asked the poor girl. She hadn't eaten for two days.

"You poor thing," said the kindly old field mouse. "You must come in from the cold and eat with me." The field mouse lived on her own in a comfortable hole and her larder was packed with good things to eat.

The field mouse was glad for company. "You can stay all winter," said the field mouse, "if you'll help me with the housework." Thumbelina was only too happy to accept, having nowhere else to go.

A couple of days later, the field mouse told Thumbelina to expect a visitor.

"He's a very dignified gentleman, is the mole," said the field mouse. "He comes to visit once a week. He's much wealthier than I am. He has a fine home with magnificent rooms. He wears a lovely black velvet coat. Now if you could get him for a husband you need never worry again."

But, Thumbelina did not want to be married to a mole.

When the mole came to visit, Thumbelina had to sing songs for him. After he had gone the field mouse would sit and chat with the girl.

"He really is a nice man," she would say. "All those big rooms, all needing a gentle female touch." Another day, patting Thumbelina's hand, she would say, "He is growing quite fond of you, you know. He would do anything to make you happy."

But one day, the field mouse said, "You know of course that he lives underground. But did you realise that he's never seen the sun or the sky and he doesn't like flowers either. He thinks they're a waste of time. He prefers worms and beetles, he says. Myself, I quite like the sun and sky but if mole chooses you, my dear, no more sun or sky for you."

Thumbelina listened to this with a sinking heart. She didn't want to go deep underground and not see the sun, or sky or flowers again.

The mole visited many times, which pleased the field mouse; "It's because of you my dear. He would never come this often just to see me."

With each visit the mole fell more in love with Thumbelina.

One day when he came to visit, he took Thumbelina and the field mouse to a passage that he had dug between the field mouse's home and his own.

"Don't be afraid," he said suddenly. "There's a dead bird in the passage." When they reached the bird, the mole poked his nose through the ceiling so that cold winter sunlight fell on the bird. It was a swallow. Its head and feet were drawn into its feathers. It had obviously died of the cold. Thumbelina was very sad. She thought it might have been one of the birds that had sung to her in the summer.

The mole pushed it with his leg. "I'm glad my children won't be like that," he said. "Singing in the summer and then starving in the winter. That's no way to live."

"You are so right," said the field mouse. "Such a waste, singing all summer and freezing in the winter. But they do say it is very aristocratic." When the field mouse and the mole turned away, Thumbelina stroked the bird's head.

That night, Thumbelina could not sleep for thinking of the bird lying in the cold passage, so she gathered some hay to take to cover it. The bird was still lying in the passage and when she had covered it with the hay she took its head in her arms. But to her amazement, the bird was not dead, it was only unconscious with the cold. As its body warmed up it began to come to life again.

Thumbelina trembled with fear. She was so small and the bird was so very big, but she drew the cover closer round the bird to keep it warm.

The next night she went to the bird again. It was much better, though still very weak. "Thank you, pretty girl," said the swallow. "I shall soon get my strength back and I shall be able to fly about in the sunshine."

"You can't go yet," said Thumbelina. "It is cold and snowing. Stay here, where I can nurse you until you are completely better." She took water to the swallow in a flower petal. When the swallow had drunk it he told Thumbelina what had happened to him.

"I tore my wing on a thorn bush," he began, "and I couldn't keep up with the other swallows as they flew south. I don't know how I ended up here. I suppose I must have crawled in for shelter."

The swallow stayed there for the whole winter and neither the mole nor the field mouse knew what was going on. When spring came and the sun started to warm the earth, the swallow was ready to leave. Thumbelina reopened the hole the mole had made and watched the swallow take flight.

"Why don't you come with me?" called the swallow. "You can sit on my back and we can fly south to the green woods."

"I cannot," said Thumbelina. "The field mouse would be most upset if I left suddenly."

"Farewell, then," cried the swallow, as it flew off into the blue sky.

Thumbelina felt very sad. With spring came the planting of the corn above the field mouse's house. It grew so high that poor Thumbelina would have become lost in such a forest, so the field mouse would not allow her to leave the house, even to sit in the sunshine.

One day the field mouse came to her. "You are to be married, Thumbelina," she said. "The mole has asked for your hand in marriage. Such luck! Now, you must start work on your clothes. You cannot go to him as a pauper."

The mole hired spiders to help Thumbelina do the spinning and weaving. Every evening the mole would come to visit her.

"I've decided that we shall be married at the end of the summer," said the mole one day.

This made Thumbelina very sad. Every morning and evening she would sit at the doorway and watch the corn blowing in the breeze. Occasionally she would catch glimpses of the blue sky.

"I wish I could see the swallow," she sighed to herself. But the swallow did not fly past. "He must be far away," she said.

Autumn came and the corn had been cut. Thumbelina's clothes were ready.

"You shall be married in four weeks," said the field mouse.

Thumbelina wept. "I don't want to marry the mole," she cried.

"What nonsense," said the field mouse. "No one will be happier, once you are married. Be thankful for your good fortune."

The wedding day arrived. The mole had already arrived to take her to live with him deep in the earth, never to see the sun again.

Thumbelina made one small request. "Please may I say goodbye to the sun and sky before we leave?" she asked the mole.

"You may," said the mole. "But please don't be too long."

Thumbelina ran outside into the field. "Goodbye, bright sun," she called, holding up her arms. She walked out into the stubble and touched a flower's red petals. "Say farewell to the swallow, if you see him," she told the flower.

"Hello, Thumbelina," called a voice from above her. She looked up. It was the swallow. He was delighted to see her. Thumbelina told him about her coming marriage to the mole.

"I don't love him," she cried. "I don't want to live deep in the earth, and never see the sun again." She could not help weeping again.

"Winter is on its way," said the swallow. "Why don't you come with me to the green woods in the south? Sit on my back and I can take you away from the mole. You saved my life, Thumbelina; let me do something for you."

"Yes, I will go with you," cried Thumbelina and she jumped up. She got onto the bird's back and tied her belt to the strongest feather. Then the bird took off and flew higher and higher leaving the mole and the field mouse far behind. The higher they flew the colder the air became and Thumbelina snuggled into the bird's soft feathers. They flew further and further south until they reached the warmer countries. Here the sun shone brightly and the sky was a brilliant blue. The scent of exotic flowers filled the air. Thumbelina was delighted.

But the swallow flew still further. Finally they landed in some old marble ruins by the sea. Vines grew around the columns. There were many swallows' nests. The swallow lived in one of them. But he didn't take Thumbelina there.

"You cannot live up here," said the swallow. "It is too high and you may fall. Choose one of these as your home."

He took her down to where a column had fallen and broken. In between grew the most beautiful white flowers. The swallow set her on one of the broad green leaves. To her surprise, there in the middle of one of the flowers was a tiny man not much bigger than herself. He wore a gold crown and had transparent wings on his back.

"Hello!" he said to the surprised Thumbelina. "Who are you?"

"My name's Thumbelina," she answered, and looking around she saw that each flower had a little man or woman in it.

"We are the angels of the flowers," said the little man. "I'm their King."

"How handsome he is," said Thumbelina to the swallow.

The little King was enchanted by the sight of Thumbelina. He took off his crown and gave it to her.

"Will you be my wife?" he asked. "And be Queen of all the flowers?"

Thumbelina said she would be very happy to become his wife.

Then out of each flower came the tiny men and women, each bearing gifts for Thumbelina. The finest gift was a pair of beautiful wings. The wings were attached to her back so that she could fly from flower to flower. There was much rejoicing and the swallow sat above them and sang the marriage song.

"Now you are my Queen," said the flower angel, "you will no longer be called Thumbelina. You are too beautiful for such an ugly name. From now on we will call you Maia."

So the flower angel and Maia lived happily to the end of their days in their white flowers. The swallows kept watch over the little kingdom among the ruins, and told the tale of the little people when they travelled around the world.

The Goose Girl

Once upon a time there lived an old widowed Queen. Her husband, the King, had been dead for some years. He had left her with a beautiful young daughter.

The girl was good and kind and she was loved by everyone. Her best and closest friend was her horse, Falada, who could speak.

When the Princess grew up she was betrothed to a Prince in a faraway kingdom. Soon the day arrived when she had to leave her home and travel to the Prince's kingdom. Her mother had many fine treasures packed for her to take to her new home. There were dishes, plates and cups of gold and silver, silks and satins for her clothes. The old Queen gave her as much as she could because she loved her daughter dearly. She also sent a maid to wait on her along the journey.

When the time came for the journey to start, the Queen took the Princess into a room. She then cut her finger with a knife and let three drops of blood fall onto a handkerchief. Then she gave the handkerchief to her daughter.

"My dear daughter, keep this handkerchief safe and it will help you out of trouble," said the Queen. The Princess tucked the handkerchief in the front of her dress.

The Queen said farewell to her daughter as she set off on her way to the Prince's kingdom. The Princess rode Falada while the maid followed behind on another horse.

After they had gone a few miles, the Princess was beginning to feel thirsty. A stream ran alongside the path, so she called to her maid.

"Please take a cup and fetch me a drink of water from the stream."

The maid just looked at her and said, "If you want water, you can get it yourself. I'm not going to wait on you."

The Princess was surprised at this but she was too thirsty to argue, so she got off her horse and went to the stream to drink. When she cupped her hands and drank, the three drops of blood said, "Ah, if your mother knew this, it would break her heart." The Princess heard them and felt ashamed, but she said nothing and got on her horse again.

A few miles further she felt thirsty again. She spoke to the maid once more.

"Please fetch me some water from the stream. I am very thirsty."

"If you want water, you can get it yourself," said the maid and she stayed on her horse.

The Princess was so thirsty she dismounted and drank again at the stream. She was very upset and surprised at what had happened. The three drops of blood said, "If your mother knew this, it would break her heart." She felt even more ashamed. She was so upset that as she leant over the water she did not notice the handkerchief slip from the front of her dress. It fell into the water and was washed away downstream. The maid saw what happened and realised that now she had the Princess in her power.

The Princess returned to the horses and was about to get up onto Falada's back when the maid said, "No, you can't get on Falada. He belongs to me now. You must ride my horse. I will be the Princess and you will be the maid." The poor Princess did not know what to do and she was forced to take off her fine clothes and give them to the maid.

"Now you must swear under the open sky that you will say nothing of this when we reach the Prince's palace, or you will be killed," said the maid to the Princess.

The maid got on Falada. The horse had been paying great attention to what was happening and he watched as the Princess got on the maid's poor horse.

They travelled on in this way until they reached the Prince's palace. When they arrived, the young Prince came running to meet them and he lifted the false Princess from Falada. She was taken into the palace with everyone cheering and rejoicing. The real Princess was left standing in the courtyard.

The Prince's father, the old King, happened to look out of the window and saw her standing there. He noticed what a beautiful and delicate girl she was. He went to the false Princess's rooms.

"Who is the girl you brought with you?" he asked. "She's standing alone in the courtyard. Would you like her sent up to be your maid?"

"Oh, no. She's only a servant girl. I brought her along for company. Now we're here it might be useful if she could be found a job outside the palace. She does like the country air but it doesn't really matter what she does." The maid was hoping the Princess would be sent far from the palace.

The King thought about it for a while. "I know," he said, "she can help Conrad, the goose boy."

"That sounds perfect," said the false bride.

The Princess was sent to work with the goose boy.

Then the false bride asked a favour of the Prince.

"The horse I rode on the way here annoyed me so much," she began, "and I fear no one else will be able to ride him. I would be grateful if you would order the horse to be beheaded." In truth, the girl was afraid the horse would say something of what he had seen.

The Prince was surprised at the request, but he agreed to give the order. The Princess heard what was to happen and she begged the man who was to cut off Falada's head to nail it to the arch she passed under when she drove the geese out into the fields. The man agreed, so the Princess could see her faithful horse every day.

Early in the morning, when she and Conrad were driving the geese through the town, she stopped in front of the arch.

"Ah, Falada, that you should hang there," she said.

Falada's head replied, "Ah, Princess, that you should pass here! If your mother knew your fate, then her heart would surely break!"

Then she passed under the arch and drove the geese out into the fields. When they reached the fields, the Princess sat down and loosened her hair. Conrad was fascinated by the long golden hair and tried to take hold of a curl.

The Princess sang a song to the wind: "Blow, wind, blow and take Conrad's hat away. Don't stop blowing until every lock is tied away."

The wind immediately lifted Conrad's hat off his head and sent it rolling down the field with him chasing behind it. When he finally caught up with it, he put it firmly back on his head. He returned to the Princess to find that she had tied up her hair so that not a loose curl was showing. This made Conrad angry. He would not talk to her for the rest of the day. In the evening they returned to town.

The next day as she passed under the arch, the Princess said, "Ah, Falada, that you should hang there!"

And Falada replied, "Ah, Princess, that you should pass here! If your mother knew your fate, then her heart would surely break!"

Afterwards when they reached the meadow, Conrad again tried to grab a curl of her golden hair but the Princess sang her song to the wind again,

at my bridegroom's side while I am forced to be a Goose Girl. If my mother knew this, her heart would surely break."

The old King was standing outside the fireplace and he heard every word the Princess said. When she finished, he called her away from the hearth.

"Bring the clothes of the Princess who is to marry my son," called the King to his servants.

The gowns were brought and the Goose Girl was dressed in them. When the King saw how beautiful she was, he called the Prince to see his true bride.

The Prince was delighted when he saw the real Princess. He had been worried about the girl who called herself his bride. She had such a cruel nature and was so selfish he feared she would never make a good wife or queen.

An announcement was then made that there would be a great feast and all family and friends were invited. The Prince sat proudly with his true bride.

The maid was brought before them and she was banished far beyond the boundaries of the kingdom.

When the old King died, the young Prince and his bride ruled their kingdom in peace and happiness.

The Ugly Duckling

Once upon a time there was a Mother Duck. She had a fine nest by a farmyard pond and in the nest there were five eggs waiting to hatch.

Mother Duck sat on the nest every day, only leaving to stretch her wings and to find something nice to eat in the pond. She waited patiently for the eggs to hatch.

One day, the first egg hatched. Out popped the prettiest, fluffiest duckling you ever saw. "Peep! peep!" he said as soon as he saw his mother.

A little while later, the second egg hatched and out popped a pretty, fluffy duckling, even prettier than his older brother. "Peep! peep!" he called to his mother and brother.

Then the third and fourth eggs hatched and two more pretty, fluffy ducklings appeared. "Peep! peep!" they called to their mother and older brothers.

Mother Duck was very happy. She had two handsome sons and two beautiful daughters. But what about the fifth egg? Mother Duck looked at it.

"Will it hatch, I wonder?" she said as she settled herself on top of it, while her new family snuggled into her warm feathers.

Later in the day an older duck swam past. "Have they hatched?" she called.

"Oh, yes," said Mother Duck proudly. "Here they are." She lifted her wings to show the four new ducklings.

"Only four?" said the duck. "I thought you had five eggs."

"I have," said the Mother Duck. "Only this one won't hatch." She stood up to show the egg she had been sitting on.

"No wonder," said the duck. "That's a goose egg. They take far too long. I'd leave it if I were you."

"Oh, I can't do that," said Mother Duck. "Not now that I've sat on it for so long."

"Oh well, it's up to you," said the other duck and she swam off. A few minutes later she came back, this time a goose was with her.

"I hear you may have one of my eggs," said the goose. "I don't understand how it could have got in your nest but can I have a look?"

The Mother Duck stood up to show the fifth egg.

"That's not a goose egg," said the goose. "That's a . . . a . . . a turkey egg, I think." She swam off, cackling to herself, "Goose egg, indeed, hmph!"

"How will I know it's a turkey egg?" called the Mother Duck after the goose.

"It won't swim," was the reply.

"Oh," said Mother Duck, and she sat down again.

"Never mind," said the other duck. "I'd leave it if I were you. There are already more than enough turkeys in the farmyard, if you ask me." She swam off muttering to herself.

But Mother Duck stayed where she was and the next day she heard the egg cracking.

"At last," she said and she stepped off to see the egg hatch. The little bird that came out was the strangest looking bird she had ever seen. It had a long neck and was covered all over with grey feathers.

"Oh," she said in surprise.

"Peep! peep!" he cried when he saw the Mother Duck.

When he was dry, Mother Duck led her brood of ducklings and the strange baby bird down to the water's edge. She walked in and listened as the ducklings plopped in behind her. She counted them as they fell in. "Plop!" "Plop!" "Plop!" "Plop!" "Plop!" 'Five!' she thought in surprise and looked back. "You can't be a turkey then, because you can swim!" she said to the last. "You must be my baby then. I suppose, now that I think about it, you are quite pretty in a way and you do swim well."

"Peep! Peep!" he replied.

Mother Duck led the ducklings across the pond to the farmyard.

"Stay close to me," she told the little ones. "Mind the big turkey and the farm cat." The little ducklings stayed as close as they could to their mother as she left the water.

"There's the grand duck," said the Mother Duck as she pointed to a fat old duck in the corner. "Now bow your heads and quack." The five little ones did so.

The farmyard ducks turned round at the sudden noise. "What! More ducks here!" they cried. Then one of them noticed the fifth duckling.

"My, my! What an ugly duckling you are!" it cried and it tried to peck at the fifth duckling.

"Don't do that!" said the Mother Duck. "He hasn't done any harm."

"Maybe not," said the duck. "But it is very ugly."

"It is certainly ugly," said the grand duck. "Can you do nothing to change it?"

"No, my lady, I can't," said Mother Duck. The ugly duckling was by now hiding behind his mother, trying to get as close to her as he could. "Besides, he may not be pretty, but he swims well. I'd say better than his brothers and sisters," she added.

"Your other ducklings are a success, my dear," said the grand duck. "But this one, I'm not so sure."

The ugly duckling, as he was now called by everyone including his brothers and sisters, spent a very miserable day in the farmyard. He was picked on by the hens as well as the ducks and had a very scary moment when the big male turkey spotted him and came rushing across the farmyard to inspect him.

"What are you?" the turkey asked.

The ugly duckling ran behind his mother, just in time to avoid being trodden on. The turkey stalked off, pecking at the ground left and right.

The second day was much the same for the ugly duckling. No one spoke to him and if they did, it was to be rude to him. Some of the ducks even tried to beat him with their wings. Some of the chickens pecked at him and the girl who came to feed the hens and ducks even shooed him away.

When evening came the ugly duckling was only too pleased to go back across the pond to the nest. He cuddled up against his mother's feathers and went to sleep.

On the third day the turkey ran up to him again, and the ugly duckling was so scared he ran through a hole in the fence and out of the farmyard in fright. He didn't stop until he reached a big lake. There he lay, cold, tired and sad until he went to sleep.

The next morning some wild ducks came to see who the stranger was.

"Who are you?" they asked. "You are very ugly, but that doesn't really matter to us unless you try to marry into our family."

The poor ugly duckling had no intention of marrying anyone. All he wanted was somewhere quiet where he could stay and feed in peace.

For two days, he was left on his own. Then two wild geese flew by. They spotted him and flew down to join him.

"If you come with us," they said, "we'll show you the way to a great lake, where there are lots of birds. They may even be friends though you are so ugly."

The two geese rose up into the air. A sudden Bang! Bang! made the ugly duckling run for cover. He saw the two geese drop from the sky like stones. They were dead. Hunters with guns were at the marsh and they were shooting at the birds as they flew up into the sky.

The ugly duckling was so scared, he could not move. He stayed by his clump of weed and waited for all the noise to stop. The shooting continued all day, but in the evening when it stopped the ugly duckling still dared not move.

When darkness fell, he suddenly jumped up and ran. He ran as fast as he could across fields. A raging storm made it difficult to see where he was going.

He soon came to a tumbledown hut. The door was almost hanging off its hinges, so he crept inside. An old woman lived there with her tomcat and a chicken.

In the morning the ugly duckling was discovered by the tomcat.

"What's this?" said the old woman. She was very shortsighted and all she could see was a fat duck. "Ooh, a duck. I hope you're a lady duck. I fancy duck eggs now and then."

The ugly duckling was allowed to stay for three weeks, while the old woman waited for him to lay eggs. But he could not lay any so finally the cat and the chicken chased him away.

The ugly duckling wandered off alone. He was so sad that no one would talk to him. "Why was I born so ugly?" he would say each day.

Autumn came and the leaves turned to yellow and brown and fell to the ground. The weather turned colder. One evening, as the sun was setting, a flock of handsome white birds flew off from the lake. The ugly duckling watched them with a funny feeling inside him. He stretched out his neck trying to copy them and gave a strange cry. He watched until they were out of sight, but he could not forget them. He didn't know that they were swans, all he knew was that they were so beautiful he loved them in a way he had never loved anyone else.

Winter drew on and it grew colder and colder. The ugly duckling had to keep swimming in his little part of the lake to stop the water freezing over. His legs grew more and more tired as he swam round in circles. At last he was too tired to swim round and lay exhausted in the water. By morning he was frozen into the ice.

Early in the morning a farmer came by with his dog. The ugly duckling made a small noise and the dog ran up to the edge of the lake barking.

The farmer had a long stick and he broke the ice around the ugly duckling.

The farmer watched as the ugly duckling crawled into some bushes to hide. There the ugly duckling stayed all winter, only coming out to find food. He waited for spring to arrive.

Time passed and soon the days grew longer and warmer. The wild birds began to return to the lake. The ugly duckling saw them but was too scared to go up to them. Instead he stretched his wings, flapped them for the first time and before he knew it he was flying above the lake.

He should have felt happy that he was flying, but he only felt sad that he was so ugly and so lonely. He flew on and on passing over moorland and fields, rivers and lakes when he suddenly saw some of the beautiful white birds he had seen in Autumn. They were on a lake below him.

He flew down and landed on the water near them. He bowed his head and swam up to them.

"Will you kill me?" he asked. "I am so ugly and so lonely, I don't want to live any more."

The swans sailed up to him with their wings outstretched.

"What do you mean?" asked one in surprise. "Why should you want to die?"

"And what do you mean by ugly?" asked another. "Have you looked at yourself recently?"

"No," said the ugly duckling, "I never look. I was always told I was ugly, so I didn't look."

"Well, look at yourself now, in the lake," said the first swan.

The ugly duckling looked and what he saw made him look up in surprise. "I look just like you," he said.

"Yes, you're like us," said a swan. "That's because you're a swan."

"A swan!" said the ugly duckling who was really a swan. "I'm a swan! Does that mean I won't be laughed at any more?"

"It most certainly does," said an older swan. "Nobody ever laughs at a swan." He swam off with his head held high.

The new swan was so happy, he just swam around talking to the other swans who welcomed him by stroking him with their beaks.

Just then some children ran down to the lake's edge.

"Look!" cried one. "There's a new swan, and they're all making friends with him. Isn't he beautiful?"

The new swan was so pleased he was beside himself with joy, but most of all he was pleased that he would never be lonely again.

Snow-White and Rose-Red

There once was an old widow, who lived with her two daughters in
a cottage in the forest. The daughters were called Snow-White and
Rose-Red because they were as pretty as the flowers that bloomed on two
rose bushes which grew before the cottage. The girls were kind, generous
and hardworking, but Snow-White was more quiet and gentle than
Rose-Red. Very often, Rose-Red would run and jump about the meadows,
looking for flowers and catching butterflies, while Snow-White sat at home
helping her mother or reading.

The two sisters loved each other dearly and agreed that they would
always be together and that whatever one had, the other would share.
They often went deep into the forest to gather wild berries but the wild
animals never harmed them. Rabbits would eat from their hands and deer
would graze at their side; goats would play beside them and birds would
stay perched on the branches as if no one were near. Because no harm ever
came to them, Snow-White and Rose-Red would often sleep on the forest
floor if they went too far from home.

Snow-White and Rose-Red kept their mother's cottage so clean, it was
a pleasure to enter. In the summer, Rose-Red would tidy the cottage, then
gather a bunch of flowers for her mother, in which she always placed a bud
from each rose bush. Every winter's morning, Snow-White would light the
fire and put the kettle on to boil. In the evenings when flakes of snow were
falling their mother would say, "Bolt the door, Snow-White," and then they
would sit down by the hearth and their mother would read to them while
they sat spinning.

One evening, when they were sitting comfortably together, there was
a loud knock at the cottage door.

"Quickly, Rose-Red," cried her mother. "Open the door. Perhaps there
is some traveller outside who needs shelter for the night."

So Rose-Red drew the bolt and opened the door. But instead of
a traveller outside, there stood a great, black bear. Rose-Red shrieked
and ran back inside and Snow-White hid under her mother's bed.

The bear, however, began to speak and said, "Do not be afraid, I will not harm you, but I am half frozen and wish to come in and warm myself."

"Poor bear!" cried the sisters' mother. "Come in and sit beside the fire." And then she said, "Come here, Rose-Red and Snow-White, the bear will not harm you, he means well." So Snow-White and Rose-Red came back and welcomed their visitor.

"Come here," said the bear, "and brush the snow from my coat." So the girls swept the bear clean as he stretched himself before the fire. Soon, they grew brave enough to play games with the bear, tugging at his fur and rolling him to and fro. When the two sisters went to bed and were asleep, their mother said to the bear, "You may sleep by the hearth if you like. It is so cold outside."

As soon as day broke, Snow-White and Rose-Red let the bear out again. From then on, the bear visited the cottage every evening. He would lie down by the hearth and allow the sisters to play with him until they grew so used to him that the cottage door was left unbolted until he arrived.

Soon spring came and everything in the forest was green and fresh. One morning the bear told Snow-White that he must leave and could not return for the whole summer.

"Where are you going, dear bear?" asked Snow-White.

"I must go into the forest and guard my treasures from the evil Dwarfs. In winter, the Dwarfs cannot work because of the cold, but in the summer when the weather is warm, they steal all they can and hide it in their caves."

Snow-White was very sad to see the bear go. As he walked away, a piece of his fur caught on the door latch and through the hole left in his coat, Snow-White thought she could see a glitter of gold. But before she could stop him, the bear ran away and was soon hidden behind the trees.

A few days later, Snow-White and Rose-Red went into the forest to gather wood. While doing this, they came to a tree lying across the path. On the other side of this they noticed something bobbing up and down. When they came closer they saw that it was a Dwarf with a long, white beard. But the end of his beard was caught under the tree and the little Dwarf was tugging hard to free himself. He glared at Snow-White and Rose-Red with red, fiery eyes.

"Don't just stand there. Aren't you going to help me?" he exclaimed.

"What have you done, little Dwarf?" asked Rose-Red.

"You stupid girl, can't you see? My beautiful beard is trapped beneath this tree and I cannot pull it free. Do something useful and help me.

Don't just stand there, gawping."

The girls tried to pull the Dwarf's beard free, without success.

"I will fetch help," said Rose-Red.

"Don't be a fool," cried the Dwarf. "There are two too many of you now. Can't you think of something yourselves?"

"Don't be so impatient," said Snow-White, and taking her scissors from her pocket, she cut off the end of the Dwarf's beard. As soon as he was free, the Dwarf picked up a sack which was filled with gold and marched off without thanking his helpers. Snow-White and Rose-Red could hear him grumbling as he went.

"Stupid girl! Both of them are idiots to think of cutting off my beautiful beard!"

Some days later, Snow-White and Rose-Red went fishing. As they neared the pond, they saw the same Dwarf hopping about on the bank.

"What are you doing?" asked Rose-Red. "You will fall into the water."

"I am hardly as stupid as that," replied the Dwarf. "But if you don't do something now, this fish will pull me in."

The Dwarf had been sitting on the bank, fishing, and his beard had become tangled in his own line. When a fish bit at the line, the Dwarf had not been strong enough to pull his beard away and the fish had pulled him forward. Now the Dwarf was holding onto the reeds and rushes by the pond and was helpless to free himself.

Snow-White and Rose-Red tried to pull the Dwarf's beard from the line, but it was no use. So Snow-White took out her scissors once more and snipped off the end of the Dwarf's beard. As she did so, the Dwarf flew into a terrible rage.

"You fool!" he shouted furiously. "Is it not enough to cut my beard once? Now look at the damage you have done. I dare not show my face to my own people anymore!" With that the Dwarf took up a bag of pearls from among the rushes and disappeared behind a rock without a single word of thanks.

Not many days later, Snow-White and Rose-Red were going to buy thread, needles, pins and ribbons from the next town. They passed over a common where there were great rocks lying about. Then just above their heads they saw a great bird flying round and round and dropping lower and lower until it flew down behind a rock. At once a piercing shriek came from behind the rock and running up to it, the sisters saw that the bird was trying to carry off the little Dwarf.

Snow-White and Rose-Red grabbed hold of the Dwarf and held onto him until the bird gave up its struggle and flew off. But instead of being grateful, the Dwarf was furious.

"Couldn't you have held me more gently? Look, you have torn my coat. Go away and stop your interfering and meddling!" With these words, the Dwarf picked up a bag filled with precious stones and slipped away to his cave among the rocks.

Snow-White and Rose-Red were used to the Dwarf's ingratitude by now, so they carried on walking into town. That afternoon as they walked home over the common, they happened to come across the Dwarf once more. Thinking he was alone, he had shaken out his bag of precious stones. The bright stones glittered in the sunshine with such a variety of colours, that Snow-White and Rose-Red stopped to admire them.

"What are you standing there for?" demanded the Dwarf, his face red with rage.

He began to shout and scream at the two girls, when a loud roaring noise was heard. A great black bear lumbered out of the forest and the Dwarf jumped up, terrified. Within seconds the bear was upon him but the Dwarf cried out, "Please spare me, great bear! I will give you all my treasures, all these precious stones, only spare my life. What have you to fear from a weak fellow like me? Look, here are two wicked girls, eat them instead of me." But the bear said nothing and dealt the Dwarf a single blow with his paw, from which the Dwarf never stirred.

Snow-White and Rose-Red began to run away, but the bear called after them. "Snow-White and Rose-Red, do not be afraid! Wait and I will come with you." Then the girls recognised the voice of their friend the bear, and stopped. Suddenly the bear stood up and his coat of fur fell to the ground. In front of Snow-White and Rose-Red stood a tall man dressed entirely in gold cloth and silk.

"I am a Prince," he said, "and I was condemned by the wicked Dwarf, who stole my treasures, to wander through the forest as a bear. Only his death would release me. Now he has received his well deserved punishment."

Then they all returned to the cottage. Soon Snow-White was married to the Prince and Rose-Red to his brother. They all shared the great treasures that the Dwarf had stolen and Snow-White and Rose-Red took their mother to live with them in their palace. In front of the palace, two rose bushes were planted and every year beautiful red and white roses bloomed.

The Princess and the Pea

There was once a Prince who wanted to marry a Princess, but he had to be certain that she was a real Princess. So he travelled far and wide to distant lands and kingdoms and on his travels he met countless numbers of Princesses. But there was always something not quite right and the Prince could never be certain that he had met a real Princess. By the end of his travels he had not found a bride so he returned home, feeling quite miserable.

One evening there was a terrible storm. Lightning flashed across the sky and thunder roared as the rain streamed down. The Prince was thinking how glad he was not to be out on such a dreadful night, when there was a knock at the palace doors. The King himself went to answer it.

As the King threw back the doors, he found a wet, bedraggled girl before him.

"Come in, come in," he cried. "You must shelter here for the night."

The girl entered the palace and stood shivering before the King and Queen. Water dripped from her hair and clothes as she shook from the cold. The King and Queen gasped in amazement when the girl announced that she was a Princess.

"But you do not look like a real Princess," said the King. The Queen, who was very wise, said nothing but she thought to herself, 'There is only one way to find out.'

As the girl warmed herself by the fireside, the Queen prepared her bed for the night. She stripped the bed of its mattress and bedclothes and on the bare bedstead she placed a single dried pea. Then, on top of this the Queen placed twenty mattresses and on the twenty mattresses, she placed twenty eider-downs. When everyone went to their rooms for the night, the girl found that she had to climb up high to reach her bed.

The following morning, the Queen asked the girl how well she had slept.

"I hardly slept at all," the girl replied. "Goodness knows what was in my bed, but I was most uncomfortable. I am black and blue. It's quite dreadful."

With that, the Queen knew that the girl was a real Princess. Only a real Princess could sleep on twenty mattresses and twenty eider-downs and still be uncomfortable because of one tiny pea. Only a real Princess could be so delicate.

On hearing this, the Prince was overjoyed. At last he had found a real Princess. The couple were married at once amid great celebration and they lived happily together for the rest of their days.

The Little Mermaid

Far out to sea, the water is as blue as cornflowers and as clear as glass.
It is also very deep and down among the depths, the sea people live.

Deep below the surface, strange plants and flowers grow and fish of all
kinds glide among them. And in the deepest part of all lies the palace of
the Sea King, with its walls of coral and roof of shells.

The Sea King lived with his mother and six daughters and it was the
youngest daughter who was the most beautiful. Her skin was pure and
clear and her eyes as blue as the sea, but like the rest of her people, she had
no legs or feet; her body ended in a fish-tail.

Each of the Princesses had their own special place in the palace garden.
One made her flowerbed in the form of a whale and another made hers
like a great sea-shell. But the youngest Princess made her flowerbed round
like the sun, which she could see when the water was calm. She was a quiet,
thoughtful child and while her sisters put the beautiful things they found in
shipwrecks, in their gardens, the youngest Princess would have nothing
except red flowers and the marble statue of a boy which had sunk with
a ship when it was wrecked.

The youngest Princess loved to hear of the world above the sea.
Her grandmother told her all she knew of the ships, towns, men and
animals, but the little Princess found it hard to imagine them because she
had never seen them.

"When you reach your fifteenth birthday," her grandmother told her,
"you can swim to the surface to sit on the rocks in the moonlight and see
the ships sailing by. Then you will see the forests and towns and all I have
spoken about."

The following year, the eldest of the six Princesses was fifteen and she
was able to swim to the surface. When she came back, she had a hundred
things to tell, but she said the finest thing of all was to lie on a sandbank in
the moonlight and look at the shore where the lights of the town shone like
stars. The youngest Princess was enchanted and longed to be fifteen herself.

The following year, the second sister was able to swim to the surface and she said the best sight of all was the sun setting, when the sky was turned crimson and gold.

When the third sister rose to the surface, she swam from the sea into a river and saw green hills and woods. In a bay, she saw a crowd of small children swimming in the water. But the sight of the mermaid frightened them, so she swam back to the open sea.

The fourth sister remained at sea where she saw ships sailing by and dolphins somersaulting in the air while whales blew great fountains of water.

Next came the turn of the fifth sister. Her birthday came in winter and she saw icebergs floating on the water and as she sat upon one of them, a sudden storm filled the sky with thunder and lightning.

Each of the sisters was delighted with the new sights they saw above the sea, but soon they grew used to them because they were able to swim wherever they wished. The youngest Princess would weep when her sisters had gone to the world above and she was left all alone.

"Oh, if only I were fifteen years old," she would cry. "I know I will love the world above very much."

And at last the little mermaid really was fifteen.

"Now you are really grown up," her grandmother told her and she put white lilies in the little mermaid's hair. The little mermaid thought how the red flowers in her garden would have suited her better, but she said nothing.

"Farewell, Grandmother," she called, as she floated to the surface.

The sun had just set when she lifted her head above the sea and there before her sailed a great ship with three masts. Music and singing came from the ship and coloured lanterns were lit along the deck. The little mermaid swam to a cabin window and there she saw a handsome young Prince. It was his birthday and everyone was celebrating. Fireworks rose high into the air, startling the little mermaid. She had never seen such sights before.

As it grew dark, the wind grew stronger and the waves began to rise higher. Dark clouds moved quickly across the sky, lightning flashed and the ship began to toss and turn on the waves. As the storm grew stronger the little mermaid realised the ship was in great danger. People were thrown overboard as the ship rolled on the sea, so the little mermaid swam closer, looking for the Prince. She saw him fall into the water and sink into the sea. So, diving deep into the water, the little mermaid swam to rescue him.

She held his head above the water and let the waves carry her to land.

The Prince was washed upon the sand and the little mermaid kept watch over him from among the waves until daylight, when a young girl found him. The little mermaid saw the Prince awaken and smile. She felt sad he didn't know that she had rescued him.

The little mermaid returned to her home beneath the waves. All she could think of was the Prince and she became even more quiet and thoughtful. At last she told her sisters of her adventure and one told her that she knew where the Prince lived.

"Follow us, little sister," said the other five Princessses and they led her to the kingdom where the Prince's palace stood.

From then on, the little mermaid would visit the palace as often as she could and she grew to love the forests and towns that she saw. But she was still unhappy and longed to walk on land and to be with the Prince. She asked her grandmother if she would ever be able to.

"The only way would be if a man loved you more than any other. Then you could live on land. When you die, instead of turning into foam upon the waves, you would have a soul that would live forever."

The little mermaid sighed and looked sadly at her fish-tail.

"Don't be so sad," said her grandmother. "This evening we shall have a court ball!"

The court ball was always a wonderful occasion. The hall where it took place was made of glass and covered with shells. Here the sea people danced to their own songs. It was the little mermaid who sang most sweetly and for a while she felt happy. But it was not long before she thought of the world above her and the Prince whom she loved so much.

She crept out of her father's palace and into her garden. There she sat, alone and unhappy while her sisters sang and danced. She gazed at the little marble statue and it reminded her of the Prince even more.

"I will go to the sea witch, even though she scares me," said the little mermaid to herself. "I will do anything to be with the Prince."

The little mermaid swam to the whirlpools where the sea witch lived. No flowers or animals lived there, only sand and bubbling water could be seen. Passing through the whirlpools, the little mermaid came to the witch's cave, which was covered in long, black seaweed. The little mermaid stopped, quite frightened, for within the depths of the cave she could see the witch and at her feet slithered sea snakes and toads.

"I know what you want," called the witch to the frightened mermaid.

"You want to be rid of your fish-tail and have legs, so that the Prince will fall in love with you." At this the witch laughed loudly. "You have come just in time."

The witch began to prepare a potion and as she did so she said, "You must swim to the surface before the sun rises and drink the potion. Your tail will shrivel and you will grow legs. But be warned, you will be in great pain and with each step that you take, you will feel as if you are walking on knives. But you will walk so gracefully and beautifully that no one will be able to move as lightly as you. If you can bear the pain, I can help you."

"Yes," said the little mermaid in a trembling voice. "I'll bear the pain."

"But once you are human," continued the witch, "you can never become a mermaid again. And on the first morning that the Prince has married another, your heart will break and you will become foam on the waves."

"I will risk anything," whispered the little mermaid.

"But you must pay me, too," said the witch. "In return for your human form, you must give me your beautiful voice."

"But what will I do without my voice?" asked the little mermaid.

"You will have your beauty, grace and eyes with which you can speak. Are you still afraid?"

"No," replied the mermaid.

"Then I will cut out your tongue," said the witch, and with this done, the little mermaid could do nothing except cry, silently.

The sea witch handed the mermaid the potion and the little Princess swam away, her heart full of sorrow. She blew a thousand kisses towards her father's palace and rose up through the dark, blue sea. She swam to the shore and pulled herself up onto the sand. There she swallowed the potion. Her body burned with pain and she fainted. When she awoke she found herself on the beach and the Prince was standing over her.

The little mermaid saw that she had beautiful legs but she still felt the pain.

"Who are you?" asked the Prince. "Where do you come from?"

The little mermaid was unable to tell him. So the Prince took her by the hand and led her to his palace. With each step the little mermaid took she felt as if she were walking on knives. But she was so happy that she did not complain.

The little mermaid was dressed in clothes of silk and gold and she was shown into a hall where she heard slaves singing for the Prince. She was sad at this because she knew her voice would have been far more beautiful.

The slaves began to dance before the Prince. The little mermaid lifted her arms and stood on the tips of her toes. She danced beautifully and the Prince was enchanted, so she danced again and again although everytime she touched the floor, she felt stabbing pain in her feet. The Prince told the little mermaid that she would always remain with him and he let her sleep on a velvet cushion outside his door.

The mermaid and the Prince went everywhere together but while others slept at night, the little mermaid would run down to the sea and cool her burning feet in the cool water. It was at these times when she thought of her family and once, during the night, her sisters came to see her.

"Little sister," they called, "come back to us. Our grandmother and father miss you so."

And as the little mermaid watched, she saw her grandmother and her father out to sea. They stretched their arms out to her but did not come near. The little mermaid cried silent tears.

Day by day the Prince grew more and more fond of her. He loved her as his younger sister, but never once thought of making her his wife.

"Don't you love me best of all?" the little mermaid's eyes would ask the Prince.

"You are very dear to me," the Prince would reply and the little mermaid would look sadly away.

One day, the little mermaid heard that the Prince was to marry the beautiful daughter of a neighbouring king.

"I must travel to meet the Princess," said the Prince to the little mermaid. "But I'm sure I won't love her as much as I love you."

The Prince took the mermaid with him on his journey across the sea and she smiled to hear him talk of storms and the mysterious things that were hidden beneath the waves, for she knew of these things far better than he did.

When the Prince arrived, the little mermaid followed him to meet the Princess. She was anxious to see how beautiful the Princess was and when she saw her, she knew that she had never seen anyone as beautiful before. The Prince fell in love with her at once, and the little mermaid felt her heart breaking.

"I am so happy," the Prince said to the little mermaid. "And you should be happiest of all for me. You are my dearest friend." The little mermaid felt very sad.

The next day, the Prince and the Princess were married as the church

bells rang. The little mermaid was dressed in clothes of gold but all she could think of was how she was going to die the following morning.

That evening, the bride and bridegroom boarded a ship that was to take them to the Prince's palace and there were great celebrations on board. The little mermaid danced before the Prince although her delicate feet felt as if they were being cut with knives. But she did not feel the pain because her heart was so sad.

When at last it was quiet aboard the ship, the little mermaid stood on the deck and looked out to sea. There she saw her sisters.

"What have you done to your beautiful hair?" her eyes cried out to them.

"Little sister," they sighed sadly, "we have given it to the sea witch so that we can help you. She has given us this knife. Before the sun rises, you must kill the Prince and when his blood flows onto your feet, you will grow back your fish-tail and become a mermaid once more. Then you can return to us." And with that, the five Princesses vanished beneath the waves.

The little mermaid took the knife that her sisters had thrown onto the deck, and she entered the Prince's cabin. There she saw him asleep, with his bride's head resting on his shoulder. The little mermaid stood in the doorway. She could not kill the Prince to save her own life. She went up to the deck once more and flung the knife far into the waves. Then she threw herself from the ship. As her body hit the water, she felt herself beginning to dissolve into foam as the sun's first rays broke across the sky.

But instead of sinking into the waves, she felt herself rising into the sky. There she saw hundreds of beautiful spirits floating in the dawn sky.

"Who are you?" she asked in a voice more beautiful than the one she had given away.

"We are the daughters of the air," said the spirits. "Through your devoted love to the Prince and your suffering you have won your soul and you shall live forever with us, as a daughter of the air."

Jorinda and Joringel

Once upon a time, there was a wicked witch who lived in an enchanted castle in the middle of a large, dark forest. By day, the witch would change herself into an owl or a cat and trick wild animals into following her back to her castle. Once there, she would cook them and eat them for her supper. At night, the witch changed back to her true form. She used her powerful magic to protect her castle, and whoever came within a hundred steps of the castle walls, would find themselves rooted to the spot and unable to move until the witch broke her spell.

One day, a young girl and boy called Jorinda and Joringel were walking through the forest. It was a beautiful afternoon and the sun shone brightly between the leaves. In the distance, Jorinda could see the walls of the enchanted castle.

"Look over there!" she called to Joringel. "What is that building?"

Joringel watched as Jorinda ran towards the castle. Suddenly he saw a large, black owl circling above Jorinda's head.

"Jorinda! Wait, don't go any nearer!" he called nervously, as he watched the owl. But it was too late. Joringel watched in horror as Jorinda disappeared. In her place appeared a beautiful nightingale. Then the black owl flapped towards Joringel and suddenly turned into an ugly, old woman with red, flashing eyes and a long, hooked nose.

"A witch!" cried Joringel and he ran towards where he had last seen Jorinda. Suddenly he found he couldn't move.

"You fool!" screeched the witch and she cackled loudly. "Your friend is my prisoner now and until I choose to break my spell, so are you!"

Joringel watched helplessly as the witch disappeared with Jorinda perched on her arm.

At midnight, as the moon cast its rays over the forest, Joringel was at last able to move. He limped away from the castle and wandered through the forest until he came to a village. There, feeling very miserable, he spent the night at an inn.

With each day that followed, Joringel would wander through the forest, hoping to catch a glimpse of Jorinda. He dared not go too near the enchanted castle in case the witch cast her spell on him again. So Joringel spent many unhappy days alone.

One night, after walking through the forest all day, Joringel had a strange dream. He dreamed he found a blood-red flower with magical powers, and in its middle was, what Joringel thought, a beautiful white pearl. In his dream Joringel picked the flower and went to the witch's castle. Everything the flower touched became free of the witch's magic and enchantment.

The following day, Joringel began his long search for the flower. "If I find this flower, then I can free Jorinda," said Joringel to himself. "And I can destroy the witch's magic."

After days of searching, Joringel finally found the flower hidden deep in the forest. It was blood-red, but instead of a pearl in its middle, there was a dewdrop.

"At last!" cried Joringel as he picked the flower, and he set off for the enchanted castle at once.

When Joringel came within a hundred steps, the magic flower stopped the witch's spell from working. He touched the castle gates with the flower and they slowly opened before him.

Joringel entered a large hall and there he heard the singing of many birds. He slipped into another room and to his amazement, Joringel found hundreds of beautiful nightingales, each one in its own cage.

'So, Jorinda is not the only prisoner the witch keeps here,' thought Joringel. 'But how will I ever find her amongst all these different birds?'

Joringel was so confused, he didn't notice the witch creep out from behind a large bird-cage.

"You!" she shrieked angrily, her red eyes flashing. "How did you get in here?" Then the witch noticed the magic flower. "Keep that away from me!" she cried, and she snatched a bird cage next to her and tried to slip through the door.

Quickly, Joringel ran at her and the cage with the flower and Jorinda suddenly appeared before him. The witch's powerful magic was at last destroyed, and she vanished into thin air.

"We must free all the other birds, too," said Jorinda, and she watched as Joringel touched each bird cage with the flower.

Jorinda and Joringel returned home together and there they were married. They both lived happily together for the rest of their days.